D1565274

A
Summer of
Silk Moths

With love to Richard Joanisse

A
Summer of
Silk Moths

Margaret Willey

flux
™
Woodbury, Minnesota

First Edition
First Printing, 2009

Book Design by Steffani Sawyer and Donna Burch
Cover design by Ellen Dahl
Cover illustration © 2009 Nenad Jakesevic
Map of Riverside and interior moth illustrations © 2009 Jared Blando

Lyrics from "Bad Moon Rising" courtesy of Concord Music Group, Inc. All Rights Reserved. Used by Permission.

Lyrics from "Black Muddy River" courtesy of Ice Nine Publishing Company, Inc. All Rights Reserved. Used by Permission.

Flux, an imprint of Llewellyn Publications

Library of Congress Cataloging-in-Publication Data
Willey, Margaret.
  A summer of silk moths / Margaret Willey.—1st ed.
    p. cm.
  Summary: A seventeen-year-old boy and girl learn long-held secrets about their pasts as they overcome their initial antipathy toward one another on a Michigan nature preserve dedicated to her dead father.
  ISBN 978-0-7387-1540-7
  [1. Secrets—Fiction. 2. Fathers—Fiction. 3. Interpersonal relations—Fiction. 4. Moths—Fiction. 5. Nature centers—Fiction. 6. Uncles—Fiction. 7. Michigan—Fiction.] I. Title.
  PZ7.W65548Su 2009
  [Fic]—dc22

                                2009019681

Flux
Llewellyn Publications
A Division of Llewellyn Worldwide, Ltd.
2143 Wooddale Drive, Dept. 978-0-7387-1540-7
Woodbury, Minnesota 55125-2989, U.S.A.
www.fluxnow.com

Printed in the United States of America

A Note from the Author about

A Girl of the Limberlost

by Gene Stratton Porter

When I was a young reader, Gene Stratton Porter's classic novel set in the Limberlost Swamp of Indiana, published a century ago, introduced me to Elnora Comstock—a wild-haired teenager with a sad situation: a long-dead father, a damaged mother, a life of poverty and neglect. Desperate for money, Elnora begins to secretly sell silk moth pupae from the woodlands around her home, using the income to pay for school books. As Elnora becomes more accomplished as a collector, she also fearlessly connects the dots of her history, eventually learning the truth about her father's death and her mother's emotional demise.

Elnora was the most adventurous, earthy girl I had ever met in a novel—curious and scientific, completely at home in the muddy swamp and, of course, obsessed with moths. I loved her! The novel came into my hands at the recommendation of my mother, who had loved the novel herself some twenty years earlier, and who knew I would fall under its spell. How many girls in the last hundred years have been inspired by Elnora Comstock's courage and heartened by her metamorphosis? How grateful I am to be in their company.

My novel, a tribute to *A Girl of the Limberlost*, is set along the St. Joseph River, close to my homeland in southwestern Michigan. In a nature preserve called Riverside, Nora arrives with an urgent need for answers to her identity. Like Elnora, she finds both information and healing in the natural world, but unlike Elnora, she has a modern teenager's anger and attitude. In bringing Nora to a place like Riverside, putting her into the care of non-parents, I acknowledge orphaned teenagers everywhere and celebrate their urgent transformations.

I am grateful to Gene Stratton Porter for bringing to life a girl for the ages. I am grateful to Fernwood Nature Center of Niles, Michigan, the prototype for Riverside.

Thanks to Richard Willey, past Environmental Educator at Fernwood and field guide, and to Serena Willey, first reader, naturalist, artist. Special thanks to my insightful editors, Andrew Karre, Brian Farrey, and Sandy Sullivan.

"I find much in life that is cruel, from our standpoints," said Elnora. "It takes the large wisdom of the Unfathomable, the philosophy of the Almighty, to endure some of it. But there is always right somewhere, and at last it seems to come."

—Gene Stratton Porter, *A Girl of the Limberlost*

Crest

Elnora's Point

Lodge & Classrooms

Visitor's Center

Animal Hospital

Main Trail

Moth Journal

Paul McMichael

Buchanan, Michigan

September 1988

Cathy and I had just left the Olde Village Inn when I saw the most amazing sight right on Main St. The upper bark of a large maple tree was pulsating with shadowy forms—it looked like the whole tree was in motion. Someone from across the street yelled that the tree was full of bats, but I saw right away that it wasn't bats, although Cathy covered her head and screamed and ran back inside the restaurant. I ran to the tree and saw that about halfway to the top were some twenty or so huge, beautiful moths in a kind of frenzy—a whole tribe of the creatures converging on one tree!

The moths were huge—their wings were the size of my little brother's hand, a kind of brownish, reddish wing with markings in red. Fuzzy orange bodies, and white stripes on the bodies. Amazing antennae. One fell from the tree to my feet and I actually picked it up and held it for a moment, before it took off and flew back to the upper trunk.

After I took Cathy home, I went back to check on Abe, but instead of taking Atlas for his usual walk around the block, I made my way back to Main St. and the same tree. The party was over and the moths were gone. It was getting late, but I was so excited that I couldn't go back home—what I really wanted to do was head into the woods near the river and search for moths. I was thinking maybe it was a special night for moths and they would be flying around everywhere in the moonlight—that's what I imagined. But I couldn't; Atlas is still too much of a little barker to take into the woods at night. So I headed home, my mind full of the sight of those vibrating moths. I need to find out what kind they were. What species would fill a whole tree like that? Huge, beautiful, slow-flying—I can't wait to ask Mrs. Shelton about it after science class on Monday.

June 2006

1. Impossible Girl

She says I was rude to her when she first came to Buchanan. She claims that the day we met I accused her of lying, but I never meant to. I was just so surprised to see a girl standing on the front porch of Abe's cabin, a place where I had never before seen a female of any age, much less one that I guessed to be near my own age, seventeen. She was wearing a tank top and pajama bottoms—the pajamas making me realize in a flash that this girl, whoever she was, had spent the night at Abe's!

And then when she told me that she was Abe's niece, it wasn't so much that I didn't believe her—there was a way I could easily have believed her, because of her red hair and how tall she was and something about her mouth, the way it curved to one side right before she spoke. In all of these ways she could easily have been Abe's niece, but there was this other way that it just wasn't possible. And so I said the thing that she would remember afterward as my rudeness, the words that set her against me at the start: "Abe never said anything to me about having a niece."

Then you should have seen the storm that worked its way across her face, turning her eyes to ice and reddening the acne on her cheeks. She had one small silver hoop in her left eyebrow; the skin around it went purple. "Well, why don't you *ask* him," she drawled nastily, "the next time you see him."

"I see him every day," I said. Then, more friendly (damage control): "My name is Pete. Pete Shelton. I work for Abe at the nature preserve—Riverside. I just came by to pick up some two-by-fours from the shed for some panels I'm building and—"

She cut me off. "Just tell him his *niece* wants to know where he keeps his television."

Before I could tell her that Abe didn't own a television, the phone rang inside the cabin and she whirled around. I could make out the stripes on her underwear through her thin pajamas. She rushed inside; the screen door slammed; she was finished with me. But because that morning was unusually hot and still, I could hear her answering the phone. "Yeah, I'm in Buchanan. Where else would I be? Has Mom called yet?"

Then, clear as a bell, I heard her add, "If you give this

number to anybody but Mom, I'll come back down there and break both your arms."

Nice girl, I thought. But I felt insanely curious. Abe's niece? I took my sweet time loading the lumber from Abe's shed into the back of my truck, hoping for another glimpse of her. But she didn't reappear.

———

As I drove back to Riverside, I replayed the scene at the cabin, trying to wrap my mind around the possibility that Abe had a for-real niece who was hanging out at his cabin in her pajamas. He hadn't said anything to me earlier that morning about a visitor. Although the truth was that Abe rarely talked at all in the mornings. Not that he was much of a talker at any point in the day—he was what my Gram called "the silent type," but I had known him practically since I was born and I was used to his silences.

I'd been working for him full-time at the nature center since the summer started. Or I should say working *with* him, since we did pretty much everything shoulder to shoulder. We were connected in lots of ways that didn't involve talking. I knew all about his childhood and he knew all about mine. I'd been hearing about his older brother Paul for as long as I could remember—Paul the science whiz, the local hero, the legal guardian of Abe who'd had died in a car accident when Abe was only thirteen. This happened a few years after Paul inherited Riverside.

It was a really tragic time. Nobody ever wanted to talk about it, which was fine with me. But it meant that Abe basically inherited Riverside when he turned eighteen. Paul's dream had been to turn the property into a nature preserve, open to the public, which suited Abe just fine. He was a naturalist too—Gram said that it was in his blood. But nobody had ever once mentioned that Paul had a daughter. It seemed an awfully big detail to have left out.

———

I found Abe sitting behind his desk, in the office that used to be the dining room of the house that—before it was in Abe's family—belonged to my grandparents, Ida and Conrad Shelton. Abe was wearing the frown he always wears when he's going over contractor invoices. He worries too much about what everything is costing, even though according to Gramps he has plenty of money.

Abe looked up from his computer screen, and I recognized the signs that he hadn't slept well—his red hair was flat on one side, frizzy on the other, and he had puffy circles under his eyes. I cut to the chase and asked, "Hey, who's the pajama girl at your cabin?"

His eyes widened in alarm. "You went to the *cabin*?"

"Abe, I told you I needed those two-by-fours today. I'm building the frames for the moth display panels."

"But you never said you were going to the cabin!"

"Since when do I report exactly where I'm going every minute? So anyway, I drive up to your front porch and this girl comes out of your cabin looking like she wants to shoot me for trespassing and she tells me she's your niece!"

"She was *up*?"

"She *is* your niece?"

Abe sat back and rubbed his swollen eyes. "She's my niece, okay? Her name is Nora. She came in on the train last night."

I flopped down behind my own desk, an oak rolltop that had once belonged to Gramps; now it was mine, and attractively littered with my latest assortment of skulls: mink, possum, raccoon, and ferret. Plus a box turtle shell, a piece of curly driftwood that looked just like a snake, and a rubber frog on a string—which I picked up and began whacking around the top of my desk.

"So, I'm driving back over here in my truck," I said, *whack*, *whack*, "and I'm realizing...I'm realizing...that if this girl is truly your niece," *whack*, *whack*, "then she has to be...she has to be Paul McMichael's *daughter*." Big *whack*. "Because you only had one brother, Abe. So who else's daughter could she be?"

Abe was now staring back at his computer screen, chewing his lip.

"Abe?"

"Right," he said. "She was. She is. His daughter."

"Abe, you never even *told* me your brother *had* a daughter!"

"No, I guess I probably didn't."

"Did you even *know*?"

He grimaced. "'Course I *knew*." He paused. "But I sure ...I didn't … I sure didn't expect … " He shook his head, at a loss for words.

"Didn't expect her to show up here?" I prompted.

He rolled his eyes to the ceiling. "Did not expect that, no."

"Where's she from, anyway?"

"Indianapolis."

"So she came on the train from Indianapolis? And you didn't know she was coming? And you just—what?—went and picked her up from the train?"

"She called the cabin, Pete. It was really late. What was I supposed to do?" But he slumped down against the back of his chair, as though it was dawning on him just how strange all of this was.

"Have you ever even seen her before?"

"No. Not since just after she was born."

"Why do you think she decided to come now?"

"I don't know exactly. It was so late and she was so tired that we didn't talk much. She was still sleeping when I left the cabin. I guess we'll be talking more about it later tonight, her and me."

Good luck, I thought, seeing that angry face again, those ice-blue eyes. "You know, she kind of looks like you, Abe." This observation seemed to startle him, so I added, "Maybe it's just her hair."

He put a hand to the back of his head, aghast.

"Does she want to stick around here for a while?"

"Oh, she's not staying," he insisted. "No, no, she's just

waiting for her mom to come and get her." But then his eyes widened in reaction to what he had just said, as though he didn't quite believe that it would work—the mother coming. His eyes met mine briefly, communicating distress. A wave of protectiveness rose in me, something that I'd felt before, even though Abe was eleven years older and taller and stronger and basically in charge of everything. He said, more to himself now, "Oh man, she can't stay with me. I have no room."

"Of course she can't stay with you. Don't even stress about it, Abe."

"She didn't sleep so great on the couch. I kept hearing her get up."

"Who cares—she's not staying! Come on, man. Don't worry about it."

But now he was rubbing the sides of his face as though his head hurt. *He's in shock,* I realized. "She came right out of the blue at you, didn't she, Abe?"

Then he looked at me. "I just can't believe this is happening."

"Hey, come on, don't worry. This will work itself out in its own way." I was quoting my Gram, an expert on the subject of trouble. Trouble came, but worked itself out. Things broke, but were rebuilt. Things got lost, but were reclaimed. Wasn't Riverside, future site of the Paul McMichael Riverside Nature Center, the best proof of that?

Abe left the office early. I escorted him out the front door of the old two-story colonial. The house was now our headquarters, and soon would be the Riverside Visitor's Center.

We headed down a newly paved walkway to our newly paved parking lot, where Abe's jeep was parked beside my ancient Chevy pickup—shiny hunter green beside rusty, bunged-up white. He climbed behind the wheel—the hardest-working man in southwestern Michigan—and Thor, his black lab, climbed into the back and gave two sharp barks: *let's go!* Abe nodded in my direction (his way of saying goodbye) and drove off with a frown, obviously dreading what awaited him at his cabin—a long-lost niece with a bad attitude.

Should I have offered to go with him? I wondered. High school had trained me well for dealing with females with attitude—I had been ignoring girls in general all that year. But the jeep was already out of sight, and I'd never gotten around to unloading the lumber from the back of my truck.

I backed as close as possible to the porch, hauled the two-by-fours out of the truck bed, and carried them down into the basement to my workshop. It was a room with cement walls and a concrete floor, wooden shelves lining each wall, two hanging swag lamps, no windows. Long ago, this same room had been Gramps' workshop. His old workbench was still there, complete with a vise at one end, a jigsaw at the other. Hanging from the wall above this were hammers, planes, drills, saws—everything totally functioning.

On the other side of the room was a drafting table, my own, where I kept my nature sketches—my drawings of flowers, birds, insects, and most recently, moths. The fact that my grandfather's workshop was my studio, even though the property belonged to Abe now, had a deep significance for me. It connected me all at once to Abe, to my family's legacy, and to Riverside. Beside my drafting table was a tarnished metal box holding twelve glass cases—Paul McMichael's moth collection.

———

I'd found the box only a few weeks earlier in a different basement—the cellar at Abe's cabin, where Abe had sent me to look for a crowbar. It was hidden on a shadowy shelf, but it caught my eye because of the label, facing outward: *Property of Paul McMichael*; and the date: *1989*. That was seventeen years ago. Too curious to resist, I'd pulled the box down, lifted the lid, shined my flashlight within, and then cried out in amazement: "Holy crap, it's the moth collection! Abe, come down here, hurry up!"

Abe found me hunkered over the box. "It's the one that won the big science fair," I said. "Gram told me about it. Look, the first-place ribbon is still here. Everything is in great condition, Abe, look—amazing condition. Look at this one!" I held up a huge, perfect *Cecropia* and shined my flashlight on it, making its eyespots flash. To my surprise, Abe visibly cringed.

"What's wrong?" I asked him.

He shook his head.

"Abe, did you forget these were down here?"

"I didn't forget," he said, recovering. "I just…I haven't thought about them in a long time."

"They're incredible, Abe—I think I'd like to draw them. And maybe down the road we could use the drawings for a brochure or a booklet or something."

"Sure, you could do that. If you want to. Go ahead. Take them."

"*Take* them?" I repeated. "Are you … like *giving* them to me?"

"If you want them, they're yours."

My head spun with possibilities. "Wow, I've been thinking I needed something new to draw this summer. Would that … would that really be okay with you, Abe? Are you sure?"

He nodded. "But keep them in your workshop," he insisted. "I don't want them cluttering up the office—there's too much going on in there already. And I'm way too busy with other stuff to help you with them. I still have the upstairs to drywall, and the River Trail is ready for clearing, and …"

He went on, listing the dozens of tasks that awaited us both that summer, but I had stopped listening. I returned the large moth to the box, clanked it shut, and hauled it with one arm by its metal handle, hurrying up the cellar stairs into the sunlight, afraid Abe would change his mind.

That night, when I told Gram what I'd found in Abe's cellar, she let the evening newspaper fall into her lap. "A metal box?" she asked softly. "Was it about this big?" She made a large square with her freckled hands. "It's a special kind of container, Peter. For preserving specimens. Conrad and I gave it to Paul after he won first place at the science fair. I always wondered what happened to it. You say it was in Abe's basement?"

"The container worked, Gram. The moths are a little bit faded, but otherwise in great shape. I took the whole collection over to my workshop at Riverside."

Gram leaned forward in her chair. "Why? Why do you want them?"

"Just … for my drawings."

"Of course," she agreed. "Drawing from life, of course." She lifted one hand to her forehead, perhaps summoning a memory. Then she asked softly, "Are you interested in moths, Peter?"

"I don't know," I said. "It was just kind of exciting to find them. Because they were Abe's brother's and all."

I waited for her to say something else, but she was silent, her head pressed against the back of her chair. Then she said, without opening her eyes, "The great silk moths used to come out of the swamps on summer nights. You could see them everywhere if the moon was right. Not anymore."

"There's a really cool *Luna* in the collection," I told her. "Huge. And some beautiful smaller moths, too."

"And the first one," she said. "*Cecropia.*" Her voice had dropped to a whisper. She was acting strange, very spacey, very un-Gram. I left her alone to finish my homework, glad that the school year was almost over and I would soon be free to spend days on end at Riverside, seeing only Abe, working side by side with him, putting in new trails on the property, finishing the classrooms, building bookcases, drawing birds and field animals and now the moths. I was feeling pretty disconnected from my friends; most of them were away for the summer, or working at camps and resorts. But it was more than that. I was avoiding people my own age, even the occasional girl who seemed interested in me. I didn't want to explain myself to strangers, didn't want anyone asking me why I lived with my grandparents, what my story was—the kind of thing that always comes up when you get to know someone for the first time.

———

A few hours after Abe left our future Visitor's Center to face his niece, I locked up the office and headed home myself. My grandparents now lived in a one-story ranch house on the northern outskirts of the property they had once owned. An acre of land, a small chicken coop, and a fenced-in garden were all they'd kept of the Riverside estate after selling it to Abe's mother when I was a baby. I had my own bedroom and bathroom and a private entrance, which suited me just fine. My grandparents had always given me plenty of space, plenty of privacy. I was lucky that way.

But that afternoon, I headed south instead of north and took Rangle Road back toward Abe's cabin, curious about what might be happening there. I slowed the truck, leaning my head out the window for signs of life. My eyes caught and followed a bright flash of hair and I saw that it was not Abe, but the girl again, moving between the house and the barn this time, hanging a pair of jeans on Abe's clothesline. She was dressed in a tube top and baggy overalls that I'm pretty sure were Abe's. Her arms, even from that distance, were white as bones. She was lifting a purple bra from a plastic bowl and clipping it to the line. *Only the clothes on her back,* I thought, my imagination working. Was she in some kind of trouble?

I slowed to a crawl, forgetting how noisy the old muffler was. To my embarrassment, the girl turned at the sound and caught me craning my neck for a glimpse of her. No doubt she recognized me from the morning. *Do I wave?* I thought. But even from that distance, the look she sent me was so unfriendly—so completely *hostile*—that I was glad I hadn't.

Moth Journal

Paul McMichael

Buchanan, Michigan

September 1988

Hyalophora Cecropia (See-Crow-Pee-Yah) are of the family Saturnidae, or silk moths, a family containing over a thousand species, all but some 200 of them tropical. And yet the huge Cecropia, the largest of the North American silk moths, is common to the swamps and forests of the Midwest—Mrs. Shelton said it would be easy to catch one near the river. Cecropia is sometimes called the Robin Moth, because of its similar coloring to the American Robin—such a fantastic, nighttime counterpart to that completely ordinary bird.

Cecropia are huge moths, with a wing span of up to six inches! The adult male's torso is orange-red and furry, banded with white. Its wings are grayish-brown with dark eyespots along the upper edge. At the center of the hindwings are pale crescent shapes called "lunules" because they look like half-moons. These neutral colors make Cecropia easily camouflaged, but I can say for sure that they are distinctive and beautiful up close, having held one in my hand.

The sexes are similar, but the males have slightly smaller bodies than the females and a more pointed torso (females are rounder), and only the males have the incredible feathery antennae that I saw on the moth in my hand. Females have a narrow, less feathery antennae.

Mrs. Shelton says there were probably a few females in the maple tree sending out pheromones (a secreted hormone) that were attracting male moths from miles away.

I have been reading everything I can find about Cecropia from Mrs. Shelton's Field Guides for Lepidopterists. She is really excited that I am interested in moths and she keeps bringing more books out of her office and letting me take them home——she has her own library! What I really want to do is go into the swamp at night and see the real thing again, a large moth in the wild; maybe even catch one and bring it to the lab, put it under a microscope, see those amazing wings up close.

2. Abe's Mistake

"So how long have you known that Abe's brother had a daughter?" I asked Gram. She was serving meatloaf, wearing a white lab coat from her teaching days that now served sometimes as an apron, sometimes as a gardening smock.

She put a thick slice onto my plate, exchanged a quick, private glance with Gramps, and then calmly asked back, "Why do you ask?"

Always answering a question with another question! "Gram! Why didn't you ever tell me that Abe's brother had a daughter?"

She lowered her small gray head, preparing a careful and accurate answer. "There was a girl born just after the accident. Named after Elnora. But we never saw her, not really.

So there wasn't much to tell. Her mother left Buchanan right after she was born."

Gramps added, "Packed up her car and sold that little house near downtown and just…took off." He made a disappearing gesture with his hands. "That was the last we saw of that one. Do you remember her name, Ida?"

"Linda," Gram said shortly, like she didn't enjoy remembering it. "From Indianapolis." She tipped her head in my direction, puzzled again. "Did Abe bring this up with you today?"

"As a matter of fact," I announced importantly, "Nora McMichael arrived all by herself last night on the train. I guess it's the first time she's ever come here. I mean, since her mom left Buchanan."

Gramps put down his fork and stared at me in disbelief. "Paul McMichael's daughter is *here*?"

Gram pressed one hand to the collar of her smock. "Her mother let her come back here?"

"Why wouldn't she?" I asked. "Her uncle lives here."

The two of them exchanged another uncertain glance. "She's with Abe?" Gram asked. "At the *cabin*?"

I pointed my fork at Gram. "Why are you so surprised? Why are you both surprised that her mom let her come here?"

"There were…many hard feelings." Gram said quietly.

"Between who?"

"Nora's mother and Abe."

"But it wasn't Abe's fault," Gramps insisted. "He was just

a boy. A boy who loved his brother more than anybody." He stopped and broke into an ear-to-ear smile. "Ida, she's forgiven him!" he exclaimed. "She's sent that little girl all this way to finally get to know her father's brother!"

Gram was smiling too. "Elnora's own granddaughter," she said. "Oh, she must be so thrilled to be here!"

I pictured Nora's face. *Thrilled* was not the word that came to mind. "How old would you say this girl is?" I asked.

"She was born a year or so after you were, Peter," Gram replied. "She must be somewhere around fifteen or sixteen."

"Not so little anymore," Gramps added. "Have you actually seen her, Peter? Did Abe bring her out to Riverside?"

"Not yet," I said. "I only saw her for like five minutes at the cabin."

"Is she tall, like the McMichaels?" Gram asked. "And pretty? Her father was so very tall and handsome."

"All I noticed was her hair," I said, dodging. I didn't want to tell them what a puffy-faced, snarling bitch she'd been.

"A redhead?" Gram guessed. "With bright blue eyes? Oh, I wonder if she looks like Elnora, Conrad. You'll just have to bring her out here, Peter, and let us see for ourselves. I can show her pictures of her grandmother as a girl. Elnora and I … we were—"

"Best friends," I finished. I'd heard it a million times.

Unexpectedly, Gram's eyes filled with tears. She rummaged through pockets for a Kleenex, covering both her eyes with it.

"Gram, come on," I said impatiently. Gramps patted one of her hands and I patted the other and we waited for her to pull herself together, which she did fairly quickly. She was a no-nonsense kind of person, my gram; she'd been the biology teacher at the local high school for forty years.

I dropped the subject of Nora McMichael, but noticed the two of them privately exchanging glances of joy all through the rest of the meal. I didn't have the heart to tell them that Abe's long-lost niece wasn't friendly, wasn't pretty, and probably wouldn't be around for more than a few days.

———

"So, did you talk to her?" I asked Abe the next morning as he came in. The moths were waiting for me in the basement, but I'd stayed upstairs to watch for him. He'd arrived late and looked again like he hadn't slept well.

"A little bit," he said, settling in behind his desk. "She's … she's not so easy to talk to right now."

"She must have told you *something*."

He sighed and rubbed his forehead. "Apparently there were problems. With her … parents. I guess her mom took off a few weeks ago, leaving Nora and her little sister with her stepdad."

"Taking a pretty big chance, wasn't she? Just assuming you would take her in when you've never even met her?"

He agreed quietly. "Yeah, she took a big chance, coming here."

"How did she even know where to find you?"

"I guess she knew I lived in Buchanan. Looked me up in a phone book at the public library and then figured out on her own how to get here. Planned it out. Made the arrangements. She's a smart girl." He sounded almost admiring. I felt a pang of unease.

"So what did the two of you do last night?"

"She needed some things. Clothes. Other stuff. She didn't bring much with her. I took her to the mall."

"Wow. Nice guy. I hope she thanked you. When I met her she wasn't acting very happy to be here."

"She's … kind of stressed out. Nervous about not hearing from her mom yet."

"So when will you bring her out to Riverside?"

"Oh, no—she won't come here. She needs to be at the cabin when her mom calls."

I couldn't hide my surprise. But Abe lowered his head, ducking my reaction, and moved into the kitchen to start coffee. I followed him to the doorway and watched him as he rummaged for filters. He was chewing his lip, ignoring me. "Are you thinking it might be weird for her to see this place?" I asked.

"I'm not thinking anything. This place isn't why she's here. And she's not staying. She's got an old score to settle with her mom."

"Right, but it just seems like she'd be a little curious."

"Well, she's not."

I let it go. It wasn't so hard to believe. She could easily have been the kind of girl who'd rather watch reality TV all day than hike a real trail or paddle a canoe. Most of the girls at my high school were like that—couldn't stand to be away from the mall, couldn't handle a few mosquito bites. And I wasn't looking. I had other things keeping me busy—Riverside projects, something new every day.

I waited for the coffee to brew, poured a cup for myself and then wandered down to the basement to study silk moths.

———

For the rest of Nora's first week in Buchanan, I made various sketches, trying several mediums (pencil, pen, a few watercolors with the more colorful specimens) and looking up information about each moth in several of the field guides Gram had given me. Every hour or so, I'd come up from the basement to check on Abe and try to get him to talk about what was going on at the cabin. "What does she do by herself all day?" I wondered aloud.

"She waits for the phone to ring. She needs a cell phone. Says she can't even go for a walk until I get her one."

"Don't buy her a cell phone!" I scolded. I knew that he had already spent way too much money on this girl, buying her a television, a comforter, an alarm clock. It was getting ridiculous.

"She's been cleaning the cabin," Abe said. "She says it helps her nerves. You can't believe how clean my place is now." He smiled.

"What do you guys talk about? Does she ask questions about your brother?"

"Not at first, but lately ..." He leaned forward in his chair, suddenly excited to tell me something. "A few nights ago," he confided, "I pulled out some of Paul's old LPs and an old turntable. She'd never really even seen an LP before—she had no idea how you play them. I told her that his favorite band had been Creedence Clearwater Revival. Then she wanted to go and play all his old Creedence. Over and over, really loud." He was smiling, proud of himself for some reason.

"You never told me that," I said. "You said his favorite band was the Grateful Dead."

"He liked them too. I just … I forgot about the Creedence thing. I haven't listened to those records since way back … way back when we still lived on Butler Street." There was something in his tone, almost a kind of gratitude. It unnerved me. Gratitude?

"You know, Abe, you could always find out yourself where the mother is and just put this girl on a bus."

"I could do that," he said vaguely.

"Well, I guess if she's going to be around a little longer, Gram and Gramps want to meet her."

This brought back his attention. "They know she's here?"

"Sure—I told them. They're all excited; they want to see if she looks like Elnora." I said this kind of mockingly, forgetting for a moment that Elnora had been Abe's mother. I hesitated, watching him; curiosity got the better of me. "So does she look like Elnora?"

He announced softly, "She reminds me of Paul."

"Paul?" I repeated. I was thinking, *the Paul who was so smart and handsome?*

"Oh yeah. Little things. The way she eats cereal. The way she sneezes. I have to work really hard not to stare at her when she talks. And the weird thing is, she doesn't even know. She has no idea that she's reminding me of him because she never knew him." He shook his head. "It knocks me out, Pete. It just knocks me out."

There it was again, the same unfamiliar tone, awe and gratitude. It made me feel something I wasn't used to feeling around Abe—excluded. The need to clarify what was unfolding at his cabin grew inside of me all that morning and through the afternoon. I couldn't shake it off. Even the hours spent in my workshop, staring at wings and antennae and striped furry bodies, did not relieve it.

———

She was picking blackberries from the bushes at the side of Abe's cabin as I approached, and I had to hide my surprise at how different she looked from that first morning. Her cheeks were clear and she'd lost the bruised shadows under her eyes and the circle of red around her pierced eyebrow. She was wearing a navy blue T-shirt and it looked brand-new—it made her eyes an intense, almost unnatural shade of blue under blond eyebrows. And she had done something different with her hair—it was shinier (or maybe just clean), with loose curls all around her forehead. I remembered my gram's question and thought maybe I *could* say that she was pretty. Improved, certainly.

But not one bit happy to see me. She held her bowl of

blackberries close to her stomach like she expected me to snatch it away, and asked, "What do *you* want?"

"Don't be so paranoid. I just need a couple of boards for a shelf I'm hanging in my workshop."

She gestured with her chin toward Abe's shed. "Knock yourself out."

Instead, I planted myself behind her. "Hey, is there some reason you're so unfriendly?"

She ignored this. But I wasn't about to give up. I took a minute to recompose my rusty charms and tried again. "So, are you enjoying your first time ever visiting Buchanan?"

"Every day, a new thrill," she muttered.

"O-kay … I'll take that as a yes. How much longer are you staying?"

"I'm leaving tomorrow."

"You are? Hey, you really should come out and see Riverside before you go. Since it's going to be a nature preserve named after your dad and everything."

I watched her arm freeze over the blackberry bush; it hung in the air a moment, the narrow back of her hand outstretched, the fingernails bitten down. "What are you talking about?" she asked.

"Riverside. Home of the almost-finished Paul McMichael Nature Center. Don't you at least want to see it?"

"*That's* what he does all day? Goes to the … Paul McMichael *Nature* Center?"

I nodded proudly.

"A nature center named after my dad?"

"Well … he was pretty important around here. People still remember him. And plus, the property—Riverside—belonged to your dad originally. Now it's Abe's. It's a hundred beautiful acres, right on the St. Joe river."

She seemed really confused now. "A hundred acres? My uncle owns a hundred acres? That my dad used to own?"

"It was the Shelton estate before that. My grandparents owned it and they named it Riverside. There's a house and a barn and a couple of outbuildings and a bunch of gardens. Abe hasn't mentioned any of this?"

She shook her head impatiently. "Where is my uncle now?"

"He's in Niles for the afternoon, seeing his lawyer about—"

"Then can *you* take me?" She pointed to my truck.

"You mean—now? Because I didn't mean now. I wasn't actually planning to—"

She put her free hand on one hip. "Look, do you want me to see this place or not? Because, seriously, I'm probably leaving tomorrow."

"All right, all right. Just let me get some boards out of the shed and then I'll drive you over there." I happened to glance down at her feet, and saw that she was wearing plastic flip-flops. Her toenails were painted the same shade of blue as her T-shirt. "You can't wear sandals," I said. It came out sounding bossier than I intended. "No, I just mean you'd be more comfortable in regular shoes. We'll be outdoors. Mud and briars. Nature. Get it?"

She rolled her eyes. "Oh, fine—just a minute."

She strode back to the porch flipping blackberries into her mouth and swishing her hips back and forth. Exaggerated swishing. She knew I was watching her. She took her sweet time.

———

"Hey, nice wheels," she said sarcastically once she had settled into my truck. She put one foot on the dash, showing me she'd changed into even more ridiculous shoes—sandals with heels.

I patted the cracked dash. "Love this baby," I said. "Not exactly in the same league as Abe's jeep, but hey—gets me where I want to go."

She didn't pretend to be interested. "So how exactly did my dad get a hundred acres on the river?" she asked.

"My grandparents sold Riverside to your grandmother, like, seventeen years ago," I explained. "And then she died and left the property to Paul. And Abe inherited it when he turned eighteen. I've been working there full time since school got out. Abe wants to have the place ready for the public in a year or so. But you know, I'm actually kind of surprised he hasn't told you any of this himself."

"He doesn't talk much, in case you haven't noticed."

She sounded critical of Abe, and I felt protective. "There's something you should know about me and Abe," I went on. "I don't just work for him. I've known him practically since I was born. He even lived with us after his brother died."

I caught myself, remembering suddenly that this brother

would be her father, a man she'd never met. I didn't want to sound unfeeling about it. I stared at the road and shut up for a minute. Then I finished. "Anyway, I'm just saying that your uncle and me—we go way back."

"Yeah, well, I go way back with him, too."

That's why you never met him until a week ago, I replied in my head. But I wouldn't have said it aloud, not that afternoon. I wanted her to understand about me and Abe, but I was also starting to see this as an opportunity to impress her. Now that she was beside me, I was noticing things—like how great she smelled and how long her legs were. I was trying not to glance too often at the front of her T-shirt, but I had secretly decided that her breasts were perfect—not too big, not too small, jiggling slightly from the bumpy road. I was determined to give her a memorable tour of Riverside, which her father had loved and which my grandparents had loved and which Abe and I now loved and which maybe she would also love. I was sure that it would at least change her opinion of me.

We were driving north on Rangle Road and we came to the small, inconspicuous sign I had made to mark the entrance to *The Paul McMichael Riverside Nature Center*, a sign that I had wood-burned and posted myself on the otherwise unmarked drive. As I slowed my truck down, I noticed that Nora was staring at the sign wide-eyed, as though she still couldn't fully believe what it said—or maybe she hadn't believed me when I said there was a nature center named after her dad just a short drive away from Abe's cabin.

"Here we are," I said unnecessarily. I turned into the narrow gravel road and drove past the birches and pines at the entrance to a stretch of prairie. The prairie grass was shimmering so intensely that I had to flip my visor down. Nora was squinting too, biting her lip and holding the dash as we bumped along.

The truck made its way along the gravel road, and then we climbed to an elevated spot from which we could see ahead of us the circle of buildings that had been the Shelton estate. Another small sign (that I had recently wood-burned) was posted just before the empty parking. It read: *I will walk alone by the black muddy river and sing me a song of my own.*

"That's from a Grateful Dead song!" Nora gasped.

I was impressed that she knew this. "Right you are. 'Black Muddy River.' One of his favorites."

She glared at me. "What the hell do you know about his favorites?"

"It's just something Abe told me."

She looked away, scowling. I pulled into the parking lot in silence, beginning to suspect that I had made a mistake, a mistake that was intensifying by the second. By the time we were walking toward the Visitor's Center, I'd upgraded my situation to full-out disaster. Nora stormed up the porch ahead of me, shoulders hunched, arms crossed tightly, wearing an expression of rage.

I tried to make feeble small talk, but she wasn't listening to me anymore. She was in her own world, soaking up the details of the office, our headquarters: the gumboots, the camera tripod, the file cabinets, the book shelves, the posters. She picked up Gram's *Peterson Field Guide to Insects* from the corner of my desk and then tossed it back, like it disgusted her. On the wall behind my desk was a framed map I'd drawn of Riverside. Nora put her face up close to it. "Who drew this?" she demanded.

"I did," I said. I lifted my hands, a little afraid she would tear it off the wall. Then she was peering at some of the other drawings I had taped to the walls—a great blue heron, an otter, a white-tailed deer—until her eyes settled on a recent photograph of our two Riverside volunteers standing side by side in the herb garden with their hoes upright. "Who are these people?"

"Christina and Bella," I said. "Our volunteers."

She pointed to another photograph on the same wall, a snapshot of a plaque that Abe had recently installed at the back of the lodge. "What's this?" She squinted to read the text. "It looks like it's somebody's name."

My heart sank.

"Whose name?" she demanded.

I didn't answer and she said, "Show me where it is."

"Maybe you should wait for your uncle, Nora. He might want to—"

"I'm not waiting for my uncle! Come on, you know everything—show me where this *is*!" And she strode past me, making me jump to get out of her way.

———

The plaque faced the prairie, reflecting the sun as we approached. Nora saw it from fifty yards away and started walking ahead of me, making surprisingly forceful strides in her ridiculous shoes. I was dragging behind her, aware that every step I took was plunging me deeper into my mistake. When Nora reached the plaque, she stopped abruptly and leaned close to it, squinting again as if trying to decipher a code. I already knew what it said; I had helped mount the plaque myself three months ago:

In Memory of Paul McMichael
1971–1991

"Okay, you've seen it," I said, speaking to her back. "Come on, Nora, let's just go see if Abe is back in the office."

At that moment, to my great relief, I saw Thor bounding through the trees, saw that Abe was not far behind him, coming at a clip, charging along in his khaki shorts and hiking boots. But when he was close enough for me to read his expression, I saw that he was in a state of dismay. He called Nora's name sharply, but she didn't turn around.

"She asked me to bring her here," I called out weakly.

"Nora?" he repeated. Then he was standing directly behind her, waiting for her to turn around.

"You weren't gonna tell me about this place, were you?" she said from between her teeth.

"I wasn't … I didn't … Nora, I just didn't know how to explain."

She whirled around. "This whole place—everything

named after him, all this *stuff*, everything you're doing out here—that office, the signs, this plaque with his name on it—Paul McMichael this, Paul McMichael that—were you even gonna *tell* me? Didn't anybody think I should *know?*"

Then she pointed to me and shrieked, "I have to find out from this *freak* here that an entire nature center named after my dad even EXISTS!"

I found my voice. "Hey, who you callin' a freak?" I yelled back at her.

"Go back to the office, Pete," Abe said. "Nora and I need to talk."

"Oh YEAH!" she cried, throwing back her head and addressing the sky. "*Now* we need to talk! *N*ow we need to tell Nora about a few things we were hoping she would never know! She would just head back to Indiana and never bother her uncle ever again and never know there was this stupid plaque on the side of this stupid building in the middle of fucking nowhere that's named after my DAD!"

Abe looked so upset that I sprang into protective mode. "Will you quit yelling at him?" I barked, making a move to get between them.

"Pete, go back!" Abe commanded. And this time it was such an unmistakable order that it made me freeze. He said it again—in a more normal voice, but still with an edge. "Go back to the office now, please."

It was the first time in all the years I'd known him that he had ever sent me away.

———

West of the pond, the Ecology Trail intersects with the River Trail and close to this intersection is a stairway made of railroad ties, a shortcut to the banks of the river. At the bottom of the stairs is a grassy crag that Abe had long ago named after his mother—Elnora's Point, a small peninsula that marks a bend in the river, just south of the docks where we bank our canoe. At Elnora's Point stands one of the first official purchases we made for the nature center—a wooden bench looking out over the water. I had carefully wood-burned Elnora's name into one of the back slats. It was a perfect spot to see cranes, herons, osprey, and even an occasional owl.

I sometimes came to the spot with my sketchpad, and sometimes just to watch the river change. Abe kept an old metal canoe parked on the riverbank; he told me that when he and Paul used to canoe from a boat slip in Buchanan, this was the place they always docked and came ashore. "I remember eating peanut-butter sandwiches right here, the two of us," he told me the day we'd carried the railroad ties down the banks. As we placed them in rows on the incline to the river, a Great Blue Heron had lifted into flight from a small patch of islands farther down the river.

"Man, I so love seeing the Great Blues," Abe had said that day. "When I was a kid, we never saw them—they were almost completely gone. Now I see them all the time. Paul would have loved that."

As lowered myself to the bench at Elnora's point, another heron lifted and disappeared—and I followed it with my eyes, hoping it would calm me. I needed something to calm me; I was panting, slightly dizzy. I was in shock from Abe's dismissal, but under the shock was something deeper. My mind was throbbing, my ears burning at the word Nora had screamed at me. Freak. *This freak here.* Why had she called me that? What did she know?

—

When I heard the sounds of Abe's boots coming downstairs to my workshop, I hunched over my sketchpad, pretending to be drawing. I had *Automeris Io* in its glass case on my drawing table. Abe stayed in the doorway for several silent moments until I looked up at him. His expression was hard to read. I considered that he might actually be angry at me.

"How was I supposed to know?" I exclaimed defensively. "How was I supposed to know you'd told her zip her about this place? You said she didn't want to come out here. But you never once mentioned she didn't even know!"

"I'm so sorry, Pete. The mistake was mine. I should have brought her out here the morning after she arrived. Hell, I should have brought her here right from the train."

His apology caught me off guard. "So … then why didn't you?"

He slumped into the doorframe and covered his eyes, upset with himself. "I don't know. I don't … I guess I was … afraid."

The word brought a memory—his face on the morning after Nora arrived, the fear I had seen in his eyes. "Afraid of what, Abe?" I asked.

"Afraid of … afraid of … how complicated it would be to

explain. Why I'm doing all this work. This work that Paul would have wanted me to do. And why I never ... made any effort to see her. To even contact her. All these years I pretended she didn't exist."

"Abe, why didn't her mom ever tell her about Riverside?"

His face clouded and he lowered his head. "I can't speak for Linda," he said. His tone was meant to stop the conversation. I studied him a moment—still leaning, clearly overwhelmed, wrestling with something inside his mind. The silence between us grew awkward.

"Where is Nora?" I asked finally.

"I took her back to the cabin."

"Abe, did you tell her anything about me? Like, personal stuff?"

"I told her you're my assistant, Pete. That's all. Why?"

"No reason. Just ... don't bring her back here, okay? I don't need that kind of drama. I have too much work to do."

"Don't judge her too hard," he said. "It's not her fault I kept her in the dark about this place." He sighed, still upset with himself. "Now I'm going to have to work really hard at getting her trust back."

"Abe, she said she's leaving tomorrow."

"Did she? She's said that every day since she arrived."

"So ... she's not leaving tomorrow?"

"Apparently her stepdad doesn't care that she left. And her mom still hasn't called her."

"But you said ... you said before that she couldn't stay with you. You don't have room—"

"She's my brother's kid, Pete. And I honestly don't think she has anywhere else on earth to go."

I had no answer to this. The thought of Nora staying longer was unbearable. So I lowered my head and pretended to be engrossed in drawing. The only sound in the room was my crosshatching pencil. Abe left the doorway. I heard the sounds of him driving away, and put down my pencil. The blue-black eyespots of the *Io* on my desk stared up at me, asking me why it mattered, why it actually hurt like hell, that some girl I didn't like, didn't care about, and hadn't even laid eyes on until a week ago, had called me a freak.

What a mysterious insect the moth is! What a completely misunderstood creature! The more I learn, the more I want to learn. Cecropia are amazing, but there are many other spectacular Saturniids living in the northern woods, gorgeous moths, moths that I can't wait to see—Polyphemus, Promethea, Automeris Io (Eee-oh), and the magnificent Actius Luna, uniquely pale green. Mrs. Shelton said that seeing one in flight is like seeing a huge airborne leaf.

It seems that the moon is some sort of navigational device for moths, although there is not total agreement on how moths react to moonlight. Different lepidopterist have different explanations. Most, but not all, believe that because moonlight is so distant, the optical illusion of light from other sources, like say a light bulb, creates a kind of disorientation in the way a moth's brain is wired—makes them confused and so more likely to exhibit the crazy flight patterns and eventual self-destruction that we humans misinterpret as a kind of "death wish." It's true that the majority of moth species cannot resist the pull of any bright light after dusk. They are sucked out of darkness by artificial light. This is why many people feel that moths are drawn to their own deaths, hence the expression: "like a moth to the flame." This, and the fact that moths are associated with night, has contributed to a sense that moths are sinister or represent something scary or unpleasant—something about death and darkness, in contrast to butterflies, which are universal symbols of innocence and hope.

Of course, this is the opposite of how I feel about moths. They outnumber butterflies by 10 to 1 and are far more diverse and mysterious.

Mrs. Shelton saw me in the lab yesterday after school and asked, "How is my favorite young votary?" She said it like it was a compliment and I pretended to know what she meant, but of course I had to look up the word later. Here is the definition:

Votary: A person who is devoted to any game, study, pursuit or religion; a devoted student or supporter.

I am a votary of moths.

3. Windows

The next morning, I came up from my workshop and saw through the office window that Abe was in the parking lot, lifting a wide, flat box into the back of his jeep. I recognized the box as the smallest of the half dozen new windows we had purchased for the lodge. "Where are you taking that?" I called through the screen.

"I made a little room for Nora at the cabin," he said, easing the box down carefully. He waved for me to come outside.

When I was beside him, I repeated, "A little room?"

"You know that space that used to be a pantry? Off my kitchen? I made it into a little room for her. All it needs now is a window."

It took me a moment to digest this news. "Well, I guess that means she's forgiven you," I said glumly.

"Oh no, she still hasn't forgiven me," Abe reported. "She still won't even talk to me. But I'm hoping we'll get past that once I move her into her own room and convince her she's welcome to stay."

"Okay, but when you say *stay* ... "

"I don't know for how long, Pete. Until she figures out this thing with her mom. One day at a time. Today we're putting in a window."

It was on the tip of my tongue to ask him if he needed my help, but I stopped myself. Because there was now the totally unfamiliar possibility that he would say no. Didn't need my help. And there was the added complication that I didn't really *want* to help. Why should I help Abe change his perfect cabin for a girl who wouldn't appreciate it? I stood at the side of the jeep, with my arms at my sides, until something else occurred to me, another jolt—I realized that Abe had come to Riverside without Thor. He never went anywhere without Thor; the dog was his shadow. "You left Thor with Nora?" I asked, incredulous.

Abe smiled. "She likes him. She remembers the lab her mother had when she was little, Thor's brother Atlas. Atlas was Paul's dog, Pete. Imagine that. Nora remembers Paul's dog."

"I thought she wasn't speaking to you," I grumbled.

"She told me this before," he explained. He meant before I'd screwed everything up, bringing Nora to Riverside. He climbed behind the wheel of the jeep, shook his head in amazement and said, "Man oh man, she reminds me so much of Paul."

I stood in the lot as he drove away, protesting silently: *How can she remind you of Paul? People loved Paul! My whole life I've heard how much everybody loved Paul. Who could love this girl?*

———

Gramps caught me studying an old photograph in the back hallway of our house—a photo I had walked by every day of my life, but never really looked at before. It was a framed black-and-white picture of two girls riding a speckled horse. The girl in front had narrow shoulders and cowboy boots and a round face—impossibly, Gram—and the other one was taller, with long legs and bare feet and a halo of curls. This girl looked strikingly like Nora, except for the way she was smiling—head tilted, eyes crescents, probably laughing. It was hard to imagine the Nora I'd met smiling like that. I hadn't ever seen her full-out smile.

Gramps came up behind me and put a hand on my shoulder. "When are you going to bring that girl around for us to meet?"

I searched my mind for an excuse and came up with the truth—something that often happened with him. "Probably never, Gramps. We haven't exactly ... hit if off."

He titled his head, as though unwilling to believe this.

"I don't like her," I insisted. "She has a really big chip on her shoulder."

"Maybe she's had the sort of life that puts a chip on a girl's shoulder," Gramps suggested.

"Meaning what?"

"Well ... I've been remembering some things about the girl's mother. Very pretty woman, high-spirited, but didn't get along with Abe. They had this trouble between them, right from the start. It only got worse after the accident. I'm honestly quite surprised that that woman would even let her daughter come back here."

"I don't think she actually did let her come here. I think it was more of a running-away kind of situation."

He lifted his eyes to mine, a level gaze. "Running away is not something that brings out the best in a person, Peter."

I turned my attention back to the photograph—two pretty girls together on horseback in what surely had been an easier time in the universe. Gramps pulled my head close to his—we were the same height—and whispered into my ear: "Bring her around, son. Do it for your grandmother."

———

The next morning, I saw that Abe had arrived at the Visitor's Center ahead of me and took it as a positive sign—a sign that things at Riverside might be returning to normal. But once inside, to my complete dismay, I found Nora herself sitting behind Abe's desk. She had the chair revolved all the way around so that her back was to me, but I could see that she was using a new cell phone, listening to someone before she exclaimed: "I heard what you *said,* I'm not stupid! If that's true, then why hasn't she called me?"

She gave the chair another spin, saw me standing in the doorway, and scowled. "Hold on a minute," she said into the receiver. Then to me: "What are you doing here?"

I kept my cool. "Last time I checked, this was my office."

"I know *that.* I mean what are you doing just standing there, eavesdropping?"

My reply was to toss my backpack from the entryway to the top of my desk—it landed with a crash, scattering bones and feathers. I found Abe in the kitchen, making a pot of coffee. "What's she doing in the office?" I demanded.

Abe's tone was calm. "She won't be long. She's talking to her sister. It looks like her mom is somewhere in the Upper Peninsula, staying with some cousins and she's trying to … "

"Abe, it's my *office.* I'm not about to start sharing—"

"Relax. I'll have her out of here in just a few minutes." He put a hand on my shoulder, reassuring me. "I'm giving her the grand tour today. She's never even laid eyes on the St. Joe River, Pete. Did you notice her shoes?"

He pushed me backwards slightly, so that I could see that Nora, still on the phone, had her long legs stretched out and her feet propped on the old radiator behind Abe's desk. Hiking boots. Heavy soles. Wool socks.

I looked back at Abe. *What has this girl done to your brain?* I wondered. Aloud, I said, "Do what you have to do, man. I'll be in the basement."

From the stairs, I could still hear Nora's voice. "Were you even *listening?* He said I can stay here as long as I want."

I entered my sanctum, took a few deep breaths in the clean dampness, and tried to block out what had just happened. For distraction, I began by putting the moth cases into rows on the floor, arranging and rearranging them and deciding how I would eventually cluster them onto display panels, all the while listening for sounds of departure above me. I wanted them gone. Gone to that river Nora had never seen. Because I was going to leave right after they did. I needed to take a drive. There was something that I needed to see for myself. Something real and concrete that would perhaps help me get a grip on what was happening to my world.

———

Never before had I walked into Abe's cabin with the feeling that I was trespassing. The cabin had always had a kind of clubhouse feeling—a clubhouse built ten years ago by Abe for a very small club, him and me. The rooms were small and low-ceilinged, with cedar beams and pine door frames, birdfeeders at windows, hardwood floors. I especially loved Abe's kitchen—all whites and hunter greens, with a pine sideboard for a table and a little pantry off to one side of the stove.

The pantry door was closed, and I gathered my nerve. Pushed it open—no more pantry. There were no shelves, no canned goods, no sacks of dog chow. I stared instead into a narrow room, almost like a train car, with a cot against one wall, a small table at the head of the bed, and a lamp and a clock on the table. The room smelled of newly sawed pine and a scent I had noticed on Nora—her fruity perfume. The bed was made, with a flowered comforter and two new pillows in ruffled cases. There was a basket of clean, new clothes in the corner. Just beyond the foot of her bed was a perfect little window, framed in new pine. It faced east, so Nora would see stars from her bed at night and wake to early sun.

Under her bed was a small, dirty gym-bag, hardly big enough for a few days of travel, empty now. Nora had gotten on a bus with only that duffel and a phone number. She'd headed north, to Abe, with no idea what sort of reception awaited her or even what sort of person he was. What kind of a girl does that? And why?

Moth Journal

Paul McMichael

Buchanan, Michigan

September 1988

I think I'm ready to find and capture real specimens now. Mrs. Shelton has loaned me one of the school's microscopes to set up at home and use in the evenings. I know she is giving me special treatment because she knows me, but I think she also sees that I am completely serious in my interest in moths and that my approach will be extremely scientific and thorough.

Cathy has been driving me crazy, calling me at least once a day to complain about the time I'm spending reading field guides about moths instead of hanging out with her. "There won't even be a test on them," she says. She doesn't understand, but I don't need her to. I don't care what anybody thinks about this. I'm a votary. Hard to explain to a non-votary. I'll be searching the dark woods

this weekend—there's some good moonlight in the fore-
cast—looking for silk moths and whatever else flies at
me, mistaking my flashlight for the moon.

4. Bella

Two weeks before Nora had come to Buchanan, our volunteers Bella and Christina had gone on a two-week road trip to celebrate Bella's ninth birthday. They had become part of the Riverside team back in March, when Christina first pulled up to the house in her old station wagon and strode up to the porch, tugging Bella by the hand. She introduced the two of them as "your brand-new Riverside volunteers." Then she told us how she and her dad used to fish along this part of the river when she was a little girl. She'd just recently moved back to Buchanan from Chicago, and when she heard the news that Abe McMichael was turning the old Shelton estate into a nature preserve, she came out straightaway to see for herself.

"I'll do anything to help you guys," she'd said that day.

She was wearing a tie-dyed smock with jeans and work boots, her hair in two long, streaky braids. "Office work, cleaning, gardening—you name it, anything you need. But mostly I love working outdoors, love it, love it, love it. And so does my Bella!" She pulled her daughter against the soft front of her, where Bella slouched and rolled her eyes, embarrassed. "This girl's a straight-A student, but she's not afraid to get her hands dirty, are you, Bella?"

Bella met my eyes, blushed, and hunched deeper. She was a really cute kid with inky black hair and huge brown eyes.

"Whatever you guys need, we want to help," Christina went on, nodding her head so vigorously that one of her dangly earrings kept bouncing against the side of Bella's face.

"We don't really know what we're doing," I confessed, happy to admit it to someone. I looked over at Abe, expecting him to agree, and saw that he was staring down at his work boots, flustered by Christina's friendliness. I had noticed before that he was extremely shy around women. But I was thrilled with the idea of having real volunteers. "If you don't mind working with a couple of amateurs," I continued, giving both mother and daughter my most masterfully handsome grin. "We'll take all the help we can get."

As soon as they had driven away, Abe griped, "What are you talking about? Amateurs?! We've had every inch of this place planned out for years!"

"Abe, they want to work here for free. And having volunteers will make our whole operation seem more professional."

"I don't care about *professional*. I don't want to be bothered with finding things for two complete strangers to do. And one of them is a little kid!"

"Leave it to me, then," I insisted. "I'll handle it. I can manage the volunteers."

And I did. I called Christina the next day and told her to come out the next Saturday. When I arrived myself that morning, there they were in the parking lot, sitting hip-to-hip on the hood of Christina's old Volvo, enjoying the first rays of springtime sun. Christina had a pair of binoculars and Bella had a birding guide propped against her bony knees. "Osprey," Bella called, pointing to the sky. I looked up. Only nine years old and already she could tell the difference between a hawk and an osprey. And that smile—ear-to-ear, all teeth like her mom's, especially adoring when it was aimed at me. From that day on, she was my shadow.

———

On their first day back from their vacation, I was so happy to hear their familiar squabbling in the kitchen that I came inside at a run and even let Christina give me one of her squishy hugs. Bella was wearing a floppy hat and I pushed it over her eyes and spun her around a few times, making her squawk with joy. My team—a reminder of the old order, the days at Riverside before a certain person had crashed the party.

"Paul McMichael's *daughter*?" Christina exclaimed when I told her what she had missed. "And Abe had never even *met* her?" She put her fingertips over her mouth in astonishment. "Oh, this must be so intense for him!"

"If Abe was *my* uncle," Bella announced with solemn authority, "I would have come to visit him before now."

"I guess there was some trouble between Abe and Nora's mom," I explained.

This made Christina scoff. "Trouble? What trouble? The man's a complete teddy bear. And he would have been— what—like thirteen?"

"Here they come!" Bella exclaimed at the office window, shushing us. "Wow, she's really tall, Mama, almost as tall as Abe. And she has the exact same color hair!"

They shambled into the office, Abe in his usual work clothes, Nora wearing ridiculously short cutoffs and those high-heeled sandals again. She had way too much make-up around her eyes, and this, along with her eyebrow stud, made her face particularly unfriendly.

"You're late!" Christina exclaimed, thrilled to see Abe, who did what he always did when he first saw Christina—stared at the floor and turned bright red.

But Nora's blue eyes flashed. "We're not *late*," she argued. "This is when we *always* get here."

"Sweetie, I'm *kidding*," Christina said, unruffled. "We're so excited to meet you! Pete told us about you this morning."

Nora flashed me dark look; I returned it.

Abe recovered enough to introduce Nora to the volunteers; then he asked Christina what she and Bella were doing at Riverside so early.

"We couldn't wait to get back out here," Bella piped up. "We missed Riverside so much. Mama says we're going to start making the River Trail today!"

"You're her *mother?*" Nora asked Christina bluntly.

Christina and Bella exchanged rueful glances. "We get a lot of that," Christina said, patting the side of Bella's brown face. "She's my big baby, all right."

Bella announced to the universe, "I'm *not* adopted, my dad is black, my mom is white, big whup."

"It's like that with me and my mom, too," Nora said. "People ask me if she's my real mother all the time because ..." Her voice trailed off awkwardly.

It was the first time I'd heard her offer a shred of personal information about herself. Even Abe looked surprised.

"I guess you take after those good-looking McMichaels then," Christina said warmly. She gave Abe an elbow in the ribs, making him blush again. This time Nora noticed and broke into a slow smile. "Your good-looking niece needs a pair of mud boots, Mister!" Christina bossed. "She can't be hitting the trails in those sandals."

"These are okay," Nora protested.

"Oh, honey, I *love* your sandals, but you'll sink into the mud up to your knees on the riverbank, trust me. We'll find you something better. Follow me." She exited, heading for the storage area, and Nora followed, surprisingly obedient. Abe disappeared into the kitchen; I could hear him humming as he opened and closed drawers, happily making coffee for the team. I was alone with Bella.

"How much did you miss me?" she asked.

"I cried every day, Bella-girl."

She threw a paper clip at me; it hit me in the forehead. "Did Abe miss my mom?"

The question surprised me. If Abe had missed Christina at all in the past two weeks, he hadn't mentioned it to me.

"Man-oh-man, did she miss *him*," Bella whispered, rolling her eyes. "She talked about him for like the whole trip. Abe McMichael this, Abe McMichael that. Drove me *nuts*."

I shushed her; I could hear Christina coming back into the office. Somehow she had talked Nora into a pair of black rubber boots that looked about three sizes too big for her. I strangled back a guffaw, which Nora caught. Bella shot me a delighted glance and said with phony sweetness, "Cool boots, Nora."

"Time to head down to the river, nature lovers!" Christina sang.

"I'm riding with Pete!" Bella called.

"Nora can ride with me!" Christina countered.

"I'm going with my uncle," Nora protested, but at that moment Abe stuck his head back into the office and announced that he had a quick errand to run in town. "Go ahead with Christina, Nora," he instructed. "Pete's in charge; he knows what to do."

Naturally, I loved hearing this. I glanced in Nora's direction to see her reaction, but she was already clomping off behind Christina in her rubber boots.

Bella eyed me sideways. "You think she's pretty?" she asked.

I pretended to think hard about it. "Well...maybe prettier than Abe."

Another paper clip came flying.

"Okay, Abe is prettier."

Another clip, then another, then a paper clip war. Finally we pulled on our mud boots, calming down. "Do you have any new drawings to show me?" Bella asked.

"Soon as we get back."

"Have you drawn any moths yet?"

"A few."

"Did you draw the one that's named after me?"

"*Isabella Tiger*—I'll do that one next. I'm taking it slow—they're very intricate creatures, Bella-girl."

"I bet you're drawing them *perfectly*," Bella insisted. She gave me her hundred-watt smile. There's nothing like a nine-year-old fan to cheer a person up after a rough week. And if she thinks you do everything *perfectly*, even better.

———

It was easy to keep out of Nora's way once we were gathered on the river. We were clearing a path through brush and pawpaw trees, laying bark in a fairly straight stretch along the eastern riverbank. Both girls stayed close to Christina, spreading bark after Christina leveled the ground. Christina was a great worker; she was strong and fast and she knew how to stay focused on a job until it was done. I worked ahead of the three of them, clearing saplings with a small axe and shoveling when necessary. It was a great day—not too hot, plenty of breeze along the river, and no bugs.

An hour into our work, I saw a pattern of tracks in the area we were grooming and stopped to identify them. The bounding pattern was clear—hind feet tracks right inside the front feet tracks. That meant mink. One of the first things Abe had taught me about laying in trails was that you never run a trail through an animal's den. Abe's rule: *the critters were here first*.

"Hold it, folks," I called out. "I see mink tracks. Scats too. There's a den nearby."

Bella echoed helpfully, "Pete says there's a mink den!"

"So what?" Nora called, annoyed.

"If there's a den, honey, then we go around it," Christina explained patiently. "Pete will scout around a moment and then we'll know for sure."

"Here comes my uncle," Nora reported, pointing up the hill. "We can ask him."

I ignored this and began scanning the nearby banks for a hole about four inches in diameter. By the time Abe made his way down to the river, I'd found what I was looking for— a small round opening in the muddy banks, surrounded by the same tracks I had seen on the path. Bella was closest to me and I waved her over. She bent close to the hole and gave a hushed cry. "It's the den! Mama, come and see!"

As Bella and I peered into the opening, we made out the tiny faces of two mink cubs, staring out at us from within. "It's a family!" Bella cried. Abe drew closer, Christina and Nora followed, and then it was the five of us, clustered around the opening, huddling to see. Abe clapped me on the shoulders and said, "Good call, man."

"Pete's a genius!" Bella trilled.

I lifted my head to catch Nora's eye over the space where Bella and Christina still crouched over the mink den. My smile was an invitation for her to join in my accomplishment. But she wasn't looking my way, and her expression was plainly astonished.

Abe called, behind me: "Let's angle the trail out a little, team. This way. Shouldn't take too long. Might need to cut down a few more saplings. I'll get a couple more axes from the truck."

While he sprinted back up the hill, I asked Nora, "Ever used an axe?"

Her tone was icy. "I think I can swing a damn axe, thank you very much."

"Oh really? Here then. Use mine." I held out my axe and she took it into both hands clumsily, holding it away from herself, obviously a novice.

I pointed to the nearest tree. "Go ahead. Let's see your technique."

Abe appeared out of nowhere and calmly stepped between us. "I'll show you what to do," he said, but first flashed me a look of some irritation. Nora also glanced at me. Through the damp curls at her forehead, the eyebrow with the metal stud in it arched mockingly.

"Thanks, Uncle Abe," she said, drawing out the word *uncle* for my benefit. I turned away from this minor setback and stayed close to Bella for the rest of the day.

Moth Journal

Paul McMichael

Buchanan, Michigan

September 1988

My first outing was pretty uneventful. I caught only a few small, common night flyers—Cutworms, Underwings, Tent Caterpillars—but I put them in jars with chlorocresol and showed them to Mrs. Shelton this morning, and she seemed excited for me. Under the microscope I saw with my own eyes the many hidden colors in those ordinary wings. Brown isn't just brown, it's purple, pink, yellow, orange—hundreds of colors are hiding in those tiny wings.

Indian summer is starting and I will try again, big flyers this time—Saturniids and Noctuidae—but Abe and his homework have me pretty busy until the weekend, so I will have to wait until Friday.

Somewhere in one of Mrs. Shelton's books, I read that some famous lepidopterist declared the Spanish Moon Moth (same family as the Luna) to be the most beautiful moth in the world. I looked at pictures of Moon Moths and Lunas and compared them. The male Moon Moth has dramatically trailing hindwing tails and also a thick furry body, but what is most dramatic about it is that the veins on its huge wings are strongly outlined in dark brown. And the eyespots! Almost an eyeball, perfectly round and unblinking. But the Actius Luna is so unique in color—that pale, iridescent green, so beautiful. No, I am sure of it—the Riverside Luna, long-tailed, broad-combed, emerald green—is the most beautiful.

The Atlas Moth of China has the largest wingspan—an impossible 12 inches! And the huge Owl Moth of India has a wing pattern resembling the face of an enormous owl. All over the world, there are gigantic moths—the mighty Hawkmoths of Australia,

Canada, and China, the Emerald Moths of Japan and Africa, the hairy Bombyx of India—all of them out there and secretly flying through trees in moonlight!

5. Fences

The next morning it was raining when I got to Riverside, so Abe declared it an "office organization day." I found myself trapped indoors with the last person on earth I wanted to be alone with. I started humming to myself to block out the fact that I was stuck with her, and once I noticed that my humming annoyed her, I was all the more inspired. For her listening pleasure, I started enthusiastically humming the Creedence Clearwater classic, "Proud Mary."

"Knock if off!" she snarled.

"It's one of your dad's favorites." I reminded her helpfully. I started humming again, getting louder as I got into the *rolling on a river* part, until she completely cracked. "Stop it!" she screamed, covering her ears. She slammed the file cabinet drawer shut with a crash. "God, you stupid freak! No wonder you don't have any friends!"

That word again. But this time I stayed calm. "I have friends," I insisted. "Lots of friends. But I've been devoting all my time to helping Abe this summer, something you wouldn't understand."

"Oh, I understand. I think there's even an expression for it … it's called *loser*."

"Not quite," I replied evenly. "A loser is more like somebody who runs away from home and nobody even cares."

It was several moments before Nora even blinked. Then she grabbed the nearest thing on Abe's desk, which happened to be an old pencil holder full of pencils, and heaved it at me. I covered my head; pens and pencils flew around me and the holder crashed against the wall. I was staring at her, open-mouthed, wondering what she would do next, when Abe poked his head back into the office. "What's going on in here?" he asked, frowning at me.

"I just dropped some pencils, Uncle Abe," Nora said, daring me with her eyes to contradict her. She began calmly picking up the ones closest to her.

"You know what, Abe?" I said. "I don't care if it's raining outside. I think I need to get out of this office."

"The rain is letting up, actually." Abe looked out the window. "I have to drive into town for my meeting, but why don't the two of you drive out to the north edge of the prairie? I've been meaning to get some fence posts set in out there all week."

I made a desperate, pleading face—*please don't send me out with her!* But Abe had already decided. "I'll get the digger and some posts and put them in the back of your truck, Pete."

One final plea. "Abe, she has no … experience."

Behind me, Nora scoffed. "Oh yeah, Mister *Experience*."

"Hey, come on, you two," Abe said. "Stop arguing and get out of here. Look, it's totally stopped raining. Go on, get some fresh air, both of you."

As I left the room to help Abe load the back of my truck, I glanced over one shoulder and saw that Nora had lowered her head and was clutching her hands together—maybe also preparing for the ordeal of being alone with me in the truck, I wasn't sure. But when she'd settled herself into the passenger side of my truck, she said crisply, "Sorry I called you a loser back there."

Her apology caught me off guard. I replied gruffly, "Sorry I said that other thing."

She smiled, but it was a forced smile; she was making a phony effort to be nice. *What's she after?* I wondered. We headed in silence for the north edge of the prairie.

———

It did feel instantly better to be outside, tooling my truck down a narrow path that cut through the prairie. The sky was breaking up, the rain changing to a light mist and patches of blue beginning to show through the clouds. A wet prairie has the most incredible smell—bergamot and heather and clean mud. I looked over at Nora and saw that she was taking in the view, still calm. She pointed to a bird perched in a tulip tree and announced, *"Phoebe!"*

I couldn't hide my surprise. She began pointing to other birds—*nuthatch, chickadee, bluebird*—naming them easily. Could she have learned this much already? "Where did you learn the names of birds?" I asked suspiciously.

"Field Biology," she announced. "Aced it last year. Surprised?"

I didn't answer. She studied my profile as I drove, staring hard and long enough to make me uncomfortable.

"So, I was wondering, Pete," she said finally, calling me by name for the first time. "How did my grandmother ever get rich enough to buy all this property in the first place?"

I had to think about this for moment, to try and recall how this had been explained to me. "Her name was Elnora. Hey, I guess you were named after her, right?"

"Nobody calls me Elnora," she insisted, the edge back in her voice. Then cheerful again, too cheerful. "So how did Elnora get enough money to buy Riverside?"

"She and my gram were best friends."

"Interesting! So how did she get ... rich?"

"Well, she became a nurse around the same time my gram became a teacher and I think I heard something once about her making all these really smart investments. And having money nobody knew about until just before she died."

"Wow, nobody knew she had money? That's just so interesting."

The falseness of her voice was really getting to me. I almost preferred her rudeness. I pulled the truck to a stop at the prairie's edge and then it was my turn to stare at her. "Yeah, it's real *interesting*," I repeated, mocking her tone. "Why don't you just tell me what you want to know?"

She looked away, frustrated. "Maybe it's not so easy, having to find out this stuff from *you*."

"Fine, agreed. It's not easy. I'm just saying you don't have to put on an act."

She still wasn't looking at me directly. I noticed her right hand, which had settled on the dashboard of my truck. Her fingers were long and thin and her nails weren't bitten down anymore. She saw me looking at her fingers and began to slowly drum them on the dashboard—the sound was surprisingly loud in the silent cab of my truck. "God, I'm already all sweaty," she said. "And we're not even outside yet."

"I can take you back if you're not up to it." I was trying to be gallant, but she took instant offense.

"I said I was *hot*, I didn't say I wasn't up to it."

I sighed, opened my door and hopped out ahead of her, not wanting to lapse back into an argument. "Let's get moving then."

"Don't start bossing me! God, I don't need you telling me what to do out here."

"Oh, so you already know what to do? With the post diggers? You're an expert on that, too?"

It was all downhill after that. I tried to show her how to handle the post-hole digger, how to set it right in the dirt, how far to push it down. It isn't difficult, but there's a certain way it has to be done. Nora balked at every suggestion. I'd never worked with anybody so unwilling to take the slightest instruction. "Just let me do it!" she kept insisting, pushing me out of the way with her hips, and then doing it wrong. Then I would show her again, and she would act as though it was my fault that she wasn't getting it right. Finally, after we'd been working on the same hole for ten minutes, I lost my temper. "Damn it, if you'd *listen* to me for once!" I yelled.

Nora looked for a moment like her head would explode. She flung the digger away from her; I watched it fall into the dirt, ruining the hole. "Fine!" she cried. "Do it yourself!"

We were eye-to-eye. Mosquitoes were hovering around our sweaty faces. "Why is it so hard," I asked slowly, "for you to accept that I know more about how things work around here than you do?"

"Why is it so hard," she asked back, evenly, "for you to stop treating me like I'm too stupid to dig a frigging hole!"

"Nobody ever said you were stupid," I said. "Although you're acting pretty stupid today!"

"You think, just because you work for my uncle, you're my boss or something? Get over yourself, Shelton. This place is the Paul McMichael Nature Center, remember? I'm Nora McMichael." She paused and stuck out her chin, wearing a mean smile, savoring a new thought. "Matter of fact, you work for *me!*"

My jaw fell. "That's crazy. My grandparents owned all of this before you even—"

"Oh please—your *grandparents*. They're not even your

real grandparents. They're just two old people who adopted you."

I couldn't hide my surprise that she knew this.

"Oh yeah, I've heard all about it," she went on. "You and your pathetic story."

"My pathetic story?" I repeated. *"My pathetic story?* You're the one who thinks you're some kind of charity case just because your dad was Paul McMichael!"

"Hey, at least I *know* who my dad was."

I couldn't believe what I was hearing. We were nose-to-nose again. I lowered my head for a long moment, struggling to control my dismay that Abe had ignored my instructions not to tell her anything about me.

"Yeah, I know all about your sad little life," Nora added. "Abe said it's why you're so awful to work with."

As soon as she said this, a calm came over me; I turned as cold as a stone. Because I knew, as well as I know my own name, that whatever Abe had told this girl, he would never, ever have described me as awful to work with. Not Abe, who had taught me the names of every bird and flower and insect in Michigan, and who'd taught me how to ride and bike and climb a tree and row a canoe. Nora was lying about Abe.

I took a step closer to her and pointed a finger calmly at the top button of her blouse. "You think you know anything about me? Well, here's what I know about you, bitch. You're basically homeless. Nobody calls, nobody wants you back. You gambled and lost and now you got *nothing*."

Nora whacked my finger away from her shirt, but I wasn't finished.

"And you're not gonna guilt-trip me or manipulate me the way you do Abe. I don't care who you are. I don't care who your dad was. I don't care what you think you know. You sure as hell don't know me. So you can quit trying to mess things up between me and Abe. Got that? Understand?"

I'd called her bluff and she knew it. She took a wobbly step backwards and then turned and started off on what I happened to know would be a very long and treacherous walk back to the office. "Want a ride?" I yelled, knowing that she would not turn around. I watched her furious strides with great satisfaction, knowing that she didn't know what she was getting into, walking through the June prairie. She would soon be navigating wicked brush, deep mud, mosquitoes, chiggers, needle-sharp burrs, and poison ivy. A nice nature hike for the city girl. Who was I to stop her?

———

The next day Abe came into the office with a long face, made coffee without speaking to me, brought a cup to my desk, and then stood in front of me with his arms crossed, waiting for me to speak. I took a sip and kept silent, making him go first.

"Okay, what happened out on the prairie yesterday?" he asked.

I fired a question right back. "Why did you tell Nora I was adopted?"

This surprised and flustered him. "Because ... you *are* adopted, Pete."

"Abe, you know I don't talk about that. And I don't like strangers knowing my business."

"She's not a stranger! She's family now. And she asked me about you; she wanted to know why you're my assistant. Then she asked me why you live with your grandparents. I didn't think it would be a big deal for me to tell her that Ida and Conrad adopted you."

"Yeah, well, it is a big deal. Did you say something to her about my dad?"

Abe looked bewildered. "Pete, what would I say? I don't know anything about your dad."

"She said something about me not having a dad. Or not ... knowing my dad."

"I don't know how she would have known that, Pete. She might have been purely guessing."

As he said it, I realized it was probably true. And I felt foolish for bringing it up. "Just don't tell her anything else about me, okay? Not one word. She'll just use it against me."

This brought Abe back to his original concern. "So what were you two fighting about yesterday?" he asked. When I didn't answer, he went on, "She walked by herself all the way back to the office, Pete. It took her, like, two hours. She got stung by a hornet on one knee and she has poison ivy on both legs."

I struggled not to laugh out loud. "Hey, I *offered* to drive her back. It was her choice to walk. Where is she anyway?"

"She's a mess. I told her to stay home."

"And you're saying this is my fault? My fault she has a temper tantrum on the prairie and totally bails on the fence posts? My fault she doesn't know how to do anything and starts screaming at me and calling me names every time I try to give her the simplest directions?"

"You should never have let her walk back by herself. You should have stopped her."

"*Stopped* her? Have you noticed how well she listens to me? Why did you have to send us out there together in the first place? Keep her out of my way, if you're so worried about her!"

I was shouting—the realization of this made me catch my breath and grit my teeth and look away. When I looked back at Abe, I saw an equally shocked expression on his face. We were having our first real argument.

Bella burst into the middle of it. "Pete—hurry!" she cried. "Mom found a baby fox on the side of the road! We think it got hit by a car—it has a broken leg! Come *on*!"

I looked back at Abe. "Go on with her," he instructed softly. "We'll talk about this later."

———

I spent the rest of the morning avoiding him, hanging out with Bella and dealing with our foundling, a baby fox with an injured right paw, dehydrated and very weak, too weak to resist handling. I knew a few basics about veterinary science from Gramps; he'd been Buchanan's only vet for nearly thirty years. With Bella's help I anesthetized the cub, cleaned and bandaged her wound, and settled her into a metal cage so that we could keep an eye on the healing process for a day or two. We named her *Canidae*, the Latin name for the family of foxes, wolves, and dogs.

We called her "Candy" for short, which Bella loved. She asked if she could use my wood-burning kit to make a sign for the cage that said *Candy*, and I showed her how to do it. She hung on every word of my instructions, and was handling the wood burner like a pro by the end of the morning.

At noon, I was eating my lunch on the porch of the Visitor's Center with Christina when Nora came riding through the parking lot on Abe's bicycle, Thor galloping happily behind her. Abe was planting beach grass along the walkway to the Center and I watched his face as Nora approached, saw that it pleased him that she had come to Riverside on her own. He gave her a two-handed, welcoming wave. She hopped off the bike, guiding it along the walkway and leaning it up against the porch. Thor bounded up to me and I put my arms around him, slapping his flanks. Nora came up the steps behind Abe in her baggy overalls, a powerful whiff of calamine coming with her. I couldn't hold back a smirk at the smell and lowered my head into Thor's coat to hide it. But not quickly enough. Nora leaned down slightly as she passed by to whisper, "Trust me, I'll get you back."

Christina, sitting beside me in one of the Adirondack porch chairs, didn't hear. She'd been watching Abe. "Wow, did you see Abe's face light up when that girl rode in?"

"He's one lucky man," I said sarcastically, but Christina didn't catch it.

"He sure seems to like having Nora around."

This I couldn't let go by. "Yeah, well, it's not like he has much of a choice."

"What do you mean?"

"I mean, like, three weeks ago she just shows in the middle of the night and announces she's homeless. What else *could* he do?"

Christina's mouth dropped. *"That's* how Nora came to Buchanan?"

"Oh, yeah. He had no idea she was coming, no warning. That first week, he didn't know *what* to do with her."

Christina sat back, digesting the information. "Wow, it's working out awfully well, if that's how it started."

"He's trying to make the best of it," I conceded. "Because she's—you know—the *famous* Paul McMichael's daughter."

Christina took a thoughtful bite out of her egg sandwich. "I knew him, you know. The famous Paul McMichael."

I was surprised. "You knew Abe's brother?"

"Well, I didn't *know* him. But I sure remember him. We all went to the same high school here in Buchanan."

"Does Abe know you remember Paul?"

She shrugged. "I mentioned right away that I grew up here. I've been kind of waiting for him to ask me if I knew Paul. Doesn't it seem like something he'd want to know about me?"

"You know how he is," I pointed out. "He doesn't ask questions."

"Not of me, anyway."

"So, what do you remember about Paul McMichael?" I asked, curious to hear a new perspective.

She tipped her head back against the wood slats of the chair and closed her eyes. "He was a few years ahead of me in school. A senior, I think, when I was still a sophomore. But it was a small high school—way fewer kids back then—and everybody knew everybody. And Paul was the sort of guy you notice. He was really something."

"I think he was my gram's all-time favorite student—a science genius."

"Oh, well, yeah, he was obviously smart, but that's not what I mean. He was so handsome! Movie-star handsome. Curly red-blond hair and the most beautiful blue eyes. A little mysterious. I knew several girls who had big crushes on him from afar. He became kind of a loner, though, once he got into that whole moth-collecting science-scholarship thing. And then he got married so young—barely out of high school, right after he inherited this place."

"So you were still around here when he got married?"

She nodded. "I was. I was a senior in high school the year he was killed. It was so tragic—unbelievably tragic. Front page in all the papers, and lots of people I knew went to his funeral. I couldn't bring myself to go. I couldn't make any sense out of the idea of him dead. And that little baby born right after … Plus, I was dying to leave Buchanan, start my new life and never come back. Or so I thought. Now here I am, fifteen years later, back in my hometown with my daughter, helping Paul McMichael's kid brother build his nature center on the St. Joe River, and meeting Nora McMichael." She sighed. "Life is so full of twists and turns, Pete. You just wait."

She took another bite of sandwich, finished with talking, but there was something else I wanted to ask her. I hesitated a moment, searching for the best way to frame a question that might sound negative: *how could somebody like Paul have a daughter like Nora?* "Does Nora seem like her dad to you?" I asked.

Just at this moment, Abe and Nora came out of the office together and passed us, heading for the parking lot. Christina put a hand up to shield her eyes from the sun and stared at their receding backs, one broad, one narrow.

"There *is* something," Christina decided. "Something about the way she carries herself. An intensity. And I suspect she's a loner too. But she's different from her father. Not as sure of herself. People loved Paul. I don't think Nora's had much experience with people just purely loving her. That's quite a difference. Know what I mean?"

"Pete!" Bella called, running toward us from the animal hospital. "Come quick! Candy is awake and she's trying to chew her bandage off!"

"To the rescue, Superman," Christina said, lifting her hands and shooing me away.

———

The same day, I drove my truck back to the prairie and finished putting in the half-dozen fence posts left over from yesterday. It was important to me to be able to point out to Abe that I was the one who had gone back to the scene of the crime and finished the job. It was hotter than yesterday, and I came back to the office in a sweat but with a feeling of righteousness—who worked harder at Riverside than Pete Shelton? Who organized everything, repaired anything, kept things moving?

When I got back, Abe was in the office on the phone and Christina was in the kitchen, washing mugs. I went to ask her where Bella was, but heard Bella's piping voice rising from the basement stairs. "Oh, he's just an *amazing* artist! I'm not kidding, he can draw anything. He's going to draw all these moths."

Then I heard another voice, asking an out-of-earshot question, and I realized with some alarm that Bella and Nora were in my workshop.

"He didn't find them *here,* Nora. He found them at the cabin. They belonged to his brother. That one who died. Oops, I guess that was your dad."

A brief silence. Then a series of new sounds—clattering wood and metal, objects being moved around. Bella's voice was suddenly anxious: "Why are you doing that, Nora? Nora, leave those alone, those are *Pete's*." And then, pleading: "Are you mad, Nora? Why are you getting so mad?"

My moths. I flew down the stairs and found that Nora was standing at my drafting table, carelessly piling the moth cases back into the metal box, causing them to clank and clatter against each other.

"Get away from those!" I cried in alarm. "They belong to me. Leave them alone!"

But she turned her back and tossed three more cases into the box, roughly, as if they were made of plastic. Something inside of me snapped. "Those are *fragile,* you idiot!" I cried. She picked up two more and I lunged across the room to grab her arms from behind. When she flailed out of my arms and turned to face me, one of the cases dropped and shattered on the concrete floor.

Bella put a hand on either side of her head and howled, "Stop it, you're breaking them!"

"Get back!" Nora screamed. "Or I'll break them all, I swear I will!"

We heard footsteps on the basement stairs and Abe came barreling into the room, Christina close behind him. "What's going on down here?" he cried.

"Bella said these were my dad's," Nora said, pointing to the half-dozen cases still on the table. "Is it true?"

"I didn't know she would get so mad about it!" Bella wailed.

"The *Cecropia*," I managed to say. I fell to my knees beside the shattered case on the basement floor.

Nora shook the surviving moth case in Abe's face. "My father had a moth collection and you just gave it away without even *telling* me!"

"It was all before you came, Nora," Abe said. I looked up at him and he gave me a helpless, trapped look.

Nora turned to Christina, who was holding Bella at her side. "Did you know about this too, Christina?" she asked. "Did everybody but me know my dad had a moth collection?"

Christina replied calmly, "None of us realized it would matter so much to you, honey."

"Matter to me?" Nora wailed. "Matter to me? I have *nothing* from my dad! Nothing!" She stared at the case that was still in her hand, a Yellow Imperial. "I didn't know anything about him! I thought he was a loser! I thought that was why my mom wouldn't talk about him!"

"Nora," Christina said gently. "We're so very sorry you thought that. Your father was a wonderful, gifted man. But you're upset. Why don't we go upstairs and I'll make some cocoa and we can all calm down a little."

Nobody moved. Christina announced more firmly, "Bella and I are going upstairs." She turned and led Bella away.

I began retrieving the broken case from the floor. The *Cecropia* was still pinned to the backing, but covered now with slivers of glass. One wing was torn, under the eyespot. With my fingers, I started picking up the larger pieces of glass, carefully, slowly, so as not to cut myself. Abe and Nora were still talking above me as though I wasn't there anymore. Or maybe I wasn't there; I felt like I had disappeared along with Bella and Christina. I heard Abe say, as though from far away, "I'll make it right, Nora. Please don't cry."

And then I heard the crushing, rumbling sounds that meant Abe had embraced Nora. I picked up another shard of glass. Above my head came Nora's voice, muffled by Abe's embrace. "They're mine, they're mine, they're mine!"

———

Half an hour later, Bella appeared in the doorway of my workshop. "You coming up?" she asked. "Mom made cocoa for you."

"Are they gone?"

"Yeah, they went back to the cabin. It's all my fault, Pete. I should never have brought her down here. I don't know why I did it. I wanted to show her something that proved you're a genius."

Through my dismay, I had to smile. "Right," I said. "You proved I'm a genius."

"Now she's going to make Abe give her all the moths. How can he *do* that?"

"Aw, they're just a bunch of dead moths, Bella. Who cares what happens to them?"

Bella wrung her hands. "Why did I *ever* bring her down here?"

"She would have found them eventually. She's always snooping around, looking for something else to get mad about."

"She doesn't *deserve* them," Bella pronounced. "She doesn't know anything about moths. She's *ignorant*."

I put an arm around Bella's shoulder. "Did somebody say something about cocoa?"

"We made it with whole milk," Bella said adoringly. "Just the way you like it." She gave me her most radiant girl-smile. And for a moment, it almost helped me to climb out of the deep, ugly hole I had fallen into. It almost did.

Moth Journal

Paul McMichael

Buchanan, Michigan

October 1988

Like most silk moths, Cecropia has an absent tongue
and cannot feed—all of its eating must happen while
in a caterpillar stage. As a caterpillar, Cecropia eats
just about anything it can crawl to in the trees and
bushes of its habitat: maple trees, apple and crabap-
ple trees, walnut, buckthorn, willow. The caterpillar then enters the pupae stage, spins a tough cocoon
to last the winter, and then hatches all through the
spring, into the late summer and sometimes, like
this year, if fall is unusually warm, adult moths can
be found as late as October. What I saw last month
on Main Street were males in a late rush to find females. And Mrs. Shelton says that it is unusual for a

mating episode to happen right in town, away from the forests and swamps. She says it might be a sign that Cecropia's habitat is shrinking.

These adult male moths live in a state of urgency—they have some two weeks to mate, and they are in a hurry. I am in a hurry to find them, determined to get back to the river every night I can get away. I invited Cathy, but she doesn't want to come with me and I'm relieved.

I must decide what to do about Cathy.

6. Rage and Ruin

Abe drove to my house that night. I knew what he'd come to tell me. But first he came inside to visit with my grandparents; they were always thrilled to see him. They had a bunch of questions about the mysteriously unavailable Nora, questions that I couldn't stand to listen to after what I'd been through that day. While he chatted with them, I went outside to Gram's backyard flower garden, my anger at Abe returning.

I needed to do something physical. Pulling weeds with my bare hands helped. When Abe finally came out into the dusk, looking for me, I pretended not to notice. I kept my eyes on the ground in front of me until the faded denim cuffs of his jeans were directly in my line of vision. "Can I talk to you for a minute, Pete?" he asked, from above me.

"I already know what you're going to say," I told him. *Dig, dig, pull.*

"I don't think you do. I don't think you understand how bad I feel about what happened today."

"I don't understand a lot of things lately, if you want the truth." *Dig, dig, pull.*

A pause. "Can I just tell you something, Pete? Can I tell you a couple of things I never told you before?"

I shrugged, but kept digging. "Sure, tell me. I can't wait."

Abe began hesitantly. "When you ... found Paul's moths back in the spring ... and you were so excited about finding them, and taking them, it was ... it was kind of a relief for me. And I didn't tell you then, but those moths ... that collection ... it always made me feel really bad. I didn't want to keep it, but I never felt right about throwing it away, either. I'd kept the box hidden in the barn at Riverside, and then once I built the cabin, I put it down the basement, out of sight where I wouldn't have to think about it. Wouldn't have to remember what was going on when it came into existence ... when my brother was a moth collector."

"What was going on?"

"It was right before our ma died, Pete."

Shit, I thought. I started digging again,

"When I saw how excited you were about finding the collection, well, I was really glad I'd kept it. I was happy for you ... happy that you were so psyched to draw the moths.

You have so much talent, Pete. It was like you were the perfect person to take them off my hands once and for all."

"I was."

"But, see … I didn't even consider that Nora existed then. I never thought about her. Hell, the last thing I expected was that she would ever show up and want anything from me."

At this, I sat back on my heels and faced him. "Well, you sure were wrong about that one, Abe. Because I'd say she wants plenty from you."

"Pete, she's trying to figure out who her dad was!"

"Fine, okay, *okay*—she's figuring out who her dad was! Fine, so you guys can sit around the cabin and talk about it for hours. Fine, even though it's pointless!" I was digging again, dirt and sand flying around me, a kind of smokescreen I was throwing up between us. "And besides, what does that have to do with something that you already *officially* gave me?"

"Things are … different now."

That was the last thing I wanted to hear. "Abe, you *gave* them to me. You said I should have them. I'm all *involved* with them!"

"I know. I know that. I know this is hard. But I'm asking you … I'm asking you to please try and understand the position I'm in. Pete, I really need to give the moth collection to Nora."

There. He'd said it. And I'd expected it. But the words actually made me rock backwards, as though he'd struck me. I lowered my head and gritted my teeth in a kind of mental pain. Abe crouched down beside me and put a firm hand on my shoulders, the pressure adding to my distress. I shook his hand away, stood up, and lurched toward the house.

"Don't go in," Abe said. "Stay out and talk to me a little while."

But I kept moving in a straight line without looking back.

"I'll see you tomorrow, okay?" Abe called.

I let the screen door slam.

On the way down the hallway to my room, Gram planted herself in front of me. "What's going on between you and Abe?"

"Nothing." I tried to brush past her.

"Peter, I know when something is wrong."

She had a certain look her in eye that meant she would not give up until she had her answer, a look that was part scientist and part something purely Gram. So I told her what had happened that day and finished with a lament: "It's just not right to take the whole collection away from me when I was already working with it! He said it himself—he said I was the perfect person to give the moths to!"

"Abe said that?" Gram asked. "What did he mean when he said that?"

"He meant … he meant … that I was the right kind of person to understand … to appreciate … "

"They did belong to the girl's father, Peter," Gram interrupted.

"She doesn't care about them, Gram!" I exclaimed. "She's

not the kind of girl who would care about a moth collection. Even if it *was* her dad's."

"What kind of girl is she, Peter?"

"She's … she's a girl who doesn't understand *anything*," I sputtered. "She would never get why someone would want to collect moths in the first place! She's just trying to get back at me. Because I refuse to put up with her insanity."

Gram listened to these accusations calmly. "You may be right about her," she said finally. "Perhaps she only wants to stir up trouble. But she's the daughter of Paul McMichael. Your newfound interest in moths doesn't change that. I expect you know exactly what you have to do."

She leaned closer, her eyes wide over the top of her glasses. I couldn't look away. "Give them to her, son," she whispered. "Be a man."

———

Even before I pulled into the cabin driveway, I could hear Abe's stereo—that's how loud she was playing Creedence. "Bad Moon Rising" was pounding out of the house, a wall of music around the cabin. I strode up the porch stairs carrying the metal box by its handle, and as I squinted through the screen, I heard another sound, a loud, motoring sound— Abe's vacuum cleaner. Nora appeared, moving between the rooms pushing the vacuum, wearing a tank top and boxer shorts, her rashy legs smeared with lotion. She disappeared again without seeing me at the door. After a moment she appeared again, and this time I saw that she was crying as she vacuumed, tears shining on her cheeks as she mouthed the words to the song: *I fear rivers overflowing. I hear the voice of rage and ruin.* Her face looked as puffy and strained as it had the first time I'd seen her. She did a half turn with the vacuum, saw my shadow at the screen, and let out a yell.

"Calm down!" I cried, but there was no way for her to hear my words above the music. I put the box down, pushed the screen door open, and strode over to Abe's stereo and turned the music off. Nora was shouting something at me the whole time, and as the volume faded I heard the tail end of it: "...scaring me half to death, and who said you could just come in here?"

The vacuum cleaner was still roaring. She fumbled for the power button and turned that off too, plunging us into silence. We stared at each other. Then I turned, went back to the screen door, retrieved the metal box and set it down on the floor between her bare feet and my work boots.

She looked down at the box, wiping her eyes roughly with the backs of her hands.

"Are they all there?" she asked.

In reply, I used my boot to push the metal box closer to her, a careless gesture.

"Including the one you broke," I said. "And just between you and me? I don't recommend that you throw them. No matter how pissed off you are because some of us won't put up with your bullshit."

Nora found her voice. "Oh my God, you think I want them just to get back at you?"

I was halfway out the door. She called to me from inside the screen, "This wasn't about getting back at you! This has nothing to do with you!"

And then one last shriek, her voice hysterical again: "I have nothing from him! I have nothing that was his!"

I never wanted to lay eyes on her again.

Moth Journal

Paul McMichael

Buchanan, Michigan

October 1988

Forceps, killing jars, chlorocresol, Glanz relaxing fluid, paper towels, insect pins, Tupperware, magnifying glass.

I think little Abe is afraid of moths.

He came down into the basement when I was spreading the two Imperials I caught over the weekend. I had relaxed them for a few days in Tupperware containers of relaxing fluid, following the instructions Mrs. Shelton found for me, and I was ready to start pinning them for display. Abe came down to tell me that he hates what I'm doing. Hates moths. Doesn't like their antennae. Doesn't like their "hairy" wings. And he especially doesn't like the way they go around and around the light until they die.

They think all light is the moon, I told him.

Then he asked me why I was sticking pins in them, if I liked them so much.

I told him it doesn't hurt them. I told him they're asleep first and then I put them in a case and they stay asleep forever.

He kept insisting that I shouldn't kill them. He doesn't really understand scientific method—how could he? He is such a gentle kid and lately he is so worried about Mom. Before he went back upstairs he gave me the last word on the subject: moths are creepy.

Is he right? Are moths creepy? A raggedy bug circling a hot lightbulb until it dies—is that creepy? Night flyers battering themselves to death against the window glass—creepy? The way they crash headlong into their own destruction?

I don't think moths are creepy. I think they're magnificent. I don't think I've ever been as excited about anything as I am about my collecting. I love being in the woods in this new way, I love tracking and waiting and hoping for and then actually finding live specimens. Yesterday I came across the two Imperials on a birch tree in the act of mating—another silk moth species, large and handsome with their yellow wings and brown eyespots. I can't wait to show Mrs. Shelton, and I can't wait to go back to Riverside—see where my membranous new friends are hiding, waiting to be part of my collection.

July 2006

7. The Trouble

For two weeks there were no more confrontations at Riverside, because neither I nor Nora said a single word to each other. This, combined with the fact that Bella and Christina were coming out almost every day and that Abe had assigned Nora to work on a separate project at the back of the house (painting some old lattices to put around the herb garden) made the atmosphere at Riverside surprisingly calm, in spite of the new, dark frame of mind I was in.

I avoided my workshop, knowing what was missing there, and instead focused all of my attention on Bella, who seemed to understand that I needed to stay away from the others. She followed me around happily and hung on every word I said. We spent hours walking the trails, taking photos of ferns and wildflowers and tending the little fox. Candy's paw was healing beautifully; she had regained her energy, which meant she needed a bigger cage. I remembered that there was a six-foot metal cage in the basement, and so Bella and I descended the stairs together and found it near the old furnace; we each took an end and maneuvered it out, passing the closed door of my workshop on the way to the stairs. Bella glanced at the door and asked, "Aren't you going to draw at your table anymore, Pete?"

"Oh, sure," I replied. "Just not today."

"Do you think you'll ever draw moths again?"

"Nope. Done with moths."

"Are you still mad at Nora?"

I shrugged, unwilling to discuss it.

"My mom said you don't understand Nora because Nora's a fighter and you're not," Bella reported. "She said Nora's a girl who doesn't know how to act around people who don't want to fight with her."

"You know what, Bella-girl? I really don't want to talk about Nora."

At this, Bella smiled a knowing smile. "You know what, Pete? That's the exact same thing I said to Mom."

———

On the second Saturday in July, Abe came into the office looking like he'd slept in his clothes. His hair was uncombed, his face unshaven. As soon as he'd poured himself his coffee, he started badgering me, asking questions about what I'd been doing for the past week, who had done what on the trails and the classrooms. I took it personally. At one point, when he asked me where all the floor plans were for the lodge (filed in the lodge folder, where they belonged), I snapped. "Did you have a rough night or something, Abe? Because I'm the guy who works the hardest around here, remember?"

There was a moment of silence, after which he said, "Sorry, Pete. Guess I'm not myself today. Maybe I should go home and go back to bed."

"Maybe you should."

But he didn't go home; he got into his jeep and headed in the opposite direction, taking the narrow road to Elnora's Point. I sat down behind my desk and at that exact moment, Nora came into the office and shut the door behind her. She paused, waiting for me to acknowledge her arrival. I did this by lifting my head very slowly, communicating great annoyance. She was standing at the door facing me, her hands still behind her on the doorknob.

"Umm ... could I talk to you for a minute?" she asked.

I hadn't been alone in the same room with her since I had delivered the moths. She was doing something different with her hair—it was pulled up and twisted into a one of those plastic clamps, with curls falling out at the sides. She was also wearing a pair of khaki hiking shorts with her new work boots. Her legs looked brown and strong.

"Pete?" she pressed.

I refocused on her face and grumbled, "Talk about what?"

"Well ... about Abe."

"Oh I don't think so. You and me? We don't need to talk about Abe."

"Please, Pete. It's … kind of important. It's … something that happened last night."

I pushed back in my chair, refusing to look up at her and making her wait for my response. But of course I was extremely curious. "Look, I have something I need to do in my workshop," I announced importantly. "If you want to talk to me, you can follow me downstairs."

She did. We descended in silence. In my studio I sat down behind my drafting table, opened a sketchpad, and began inking in a pencil drawing of the little fox for Bella. I wanted Nora to see me at my drawing table, to realize that I still owned this universe regardless of what she'd recently taken from it.

Nora settled herself onto a wooden crate on the floor and slowly stretched out her legs. Her face was troubled. I could tell that she was struggling to be patient.

"What's up with Abe?" I asked finally.

"My mom called last night," Nora replied. "I've been here over a month and *finally* she calls. First she talks to me. Or I should say, she screams at me. Then she tells me to put Abe on. From what I could tell, she was blaming him for the fact that I'm here. Like this must have been all his idea."

"Why would she think that?"

"I don't know why. But I could tell it was really upsetting him. He kept repeating that he had no idea I was coming. Then he told her that he wasn't going to send me back to Indianapolis if she wasn't there. Then all of a sudden, he hung up on her. He just slammed the phone down. I don't know what she'd said before he did that. I was watching him and he turned to me and gave me this *look,* this kind of scared look, like he wasn't sure that he was going to be able to handle whatever happens next."

I knew that look. "So, what did happen next?"

"He went into his bedroom and shut the door. I waited for him for a little while, and then I gave up and went to bed. This morning I tried to get him to talk about it, but he told me he wasn't going to talk about my mom. Like he wouldn't bad-mouth her in front of me."

"So you want me to find out what your mom said?"

She nodded hopefully. "Find out what the trouble is between them."

Trouble. The same word Gramps and Gram had used recently, talking about the past. Hearing it from Nora inspired me to make a counteroffer. "Look, my grandparents want to meet you. They ask me—like, every day—why I haven't brought you over yet to see them. I'll talk to Abe if you'll come over and meet them."

Nora seemed unsurprised. "Yeah, yeah, Abe keeps bugging me about that too."

"I'm tired of making excuses. Could you please just ride your bike over tonight and pretend you care and get it over with?"

She thought a moment. "Do they know how much you hate me?"

Her bluntness surprised me. "They know nothing."

"Will you be there?"

"I live there, remember? In a pathetic state, with my not-real grandparents."

"Look, I'm sorry I said that, okay? God, you said some pretty evil stuff that day too." She stood up, turned her back, and dusted off the seat of her shorts, preparing to leave.

"So you're coming over?"

She arched the studded eyebrow. "Once you talk to Abe."

"I'll talk to him as soon as I can find him."

"He's at the river," she reported. "He goes down there sometimes to think. Sits on that bench named after his mom."

She said this like it would be news to me—it annoyed me so much I could have thrown something at her. After she'd sauntered out, I looked down at my drawing, and saw that a huge blob of ink had dripped from my pen onto the fox's tail, ruining everything.

———

I hadn't had a real conversation with Abe in a while, either. The truth was, I'd been punishing him by keeping him at arm's length. But when I spied him hunched on the bench at Elnora's Point with his head in his hands, all I wanted in the world was to cheer him up. "Guess what?" I called from the crest above him. "Nora's coming over tonight to meet Gram and Gramps!"

Abe lifted his face and smiled. "Seriously? I've been bugging her about that for weeks. How did you get her to say yes?"

I came closer, taking the railroad ties two at a time. "I just asked her."

"Wow, I am truly glad to hear that. I was hoping the two of you could start getting along a little better."

I sat down beside him and clapped a hand on his back. "Yeah, no problem. We had a good talk and she was telling me about a certain unpleasant phone call you had last night."

Abe's eyes widened in amazement. "She told you about that?"

"Sure, sure, we talked about it. Nora said her mom was blaming you for her being here."

I watched Abe's profile, saw his jaw tightening as he looked out over the river. "She said I had it planned all along. But I had no plan. The thought never even entered my mind."

"Of course it didn't," I agreed.

"But why *didn't* I have a plan, Pete? A plan to get my brother's kid out here and let her see for herself what her father's life was all about. The things that mattered to him. The things he wanted from this place. Jesus, I can't believe I went so long without ever even *trying*."

He sounded really down on himself. I gave his shoulder a bolstering thump. "Come on, Abe. It's not like she ever tried to contact *you*."

"She was just a kid," Abe argued sadly. "A little kid with a mom who didn't want my name even mentioned."

"Why not?" I prompted. "What does she have against you anyway?"

He leaned forward into a slouch again, talking more to himself now. "Man, I should have known this would happen. It was only a matter of time. I should have been more prepared. But she said she would never come back here. It just never occurred to me that Nora might come without her."

"Abe, why did Nora's mom say she would never come back here?"

A pause. A deep sigh. "There was this lawsuit, see. After Paul died ... this big, ugly lawsuit. Because she ... Linda ... she wanted half of Riverside for herself."

"Half of *Riverside*?" I repeated.

"She would have sold it. But Paul had already set up the will so that all the property would go to me when I turned eighteen. So Linda sued. Six months after the accident, she got a lawyer and challenged the will and I had to go to court. I was thirteen, Pete. I had nobody to help me, no family left, only Ida and Conrad; they were still taking care of Riverside."

"But ... you won!"

"Oh, I won, Pete. I won big. Everybody was so happy for me. And I didn't care that Linda left and took the baby with her. I wanted them gone. I wanted the whole mess to be over. And then I wanted everyone in this town to just leave me alone." He turned to me and his voice fell to a whisper. "Except for you, Pete. You were what kept me going back then. You were the greatest little kid. So smart and funny, always following me around, always cheering me up. Kind of like you and Bella. That's how you were to me. Ida and Conrad helped me too, of course, but it was mostly you."

Abe had never said anything so personal to me before. I scanned the river, hiding what I was feeling, some of it guilt for how I'd been treating him. A trio of crows broke into noise above us; they were chasing a Cooper's Hawk. It was an aerial performance that we watched together in silent appreciation.

When the birds were gone, Abe spoke again. "There's a lot of things from back then that I never told anybody. Things I haven't allowed myself to think about in a long time. Not until Nora came and started asking me questions about her dad."

He cleared his throat, and I sensed he was about to change the subject. "Anyway, I'm really glad Nora's going to finally meet Ida and Conrad," he said. "They'll make her feel welcome. She needs to feel welcome around here, Pete; it'll change her. It's already changing her. But I guess you know that."

"Right." I stood up to leave, but remembered my original assignment. "So, what was it exactly that Nora's mom said to you last night? Before you hung up on her?"

"It doesn't matter," he said. "She won't ever come back here."

I didn't press him—I'd learned what Nora really wanted to know. It appeared that the root of the trouble between

Abe and his brother's wife was a lawsuit over a parcel of land that was worth money. A lot of money. I had a feeling this was something Nora would understand.

———

Gramps and I were outside feeding chickens when I saw a flash of red hair against the pink sunset on the horizon—someone on a bicycle, turning into the drive. I hadn't told Gramps Nora was coming, in case she changed her mind. He put a hand over his eyes to shield them from the sunset as Nora came closer. Halfway up the drive, she hopped off the bike and walked the rest of the way. Her hair, with the sunset behind it, seemed almost aflame.

"I'm Nora," she called. All her attention was on Gramps; she didn't even look at me. I took the bike out of her hands and leaned it against the fence that bordered the chicken yard. Gramps stepped between us, clasped one of Nora's hands, and found his voice. "Oh, my word, of course you are! I'd have known you anywhere! Pete never mentioned that you'd be coming by this evening!"

"I wasn't sure she'd show up," I explained. Nora sent me a sidelong glance of irritation.

"Nora McMichael, for heaven's sake, let me look at you," Gramps exclaimed, still pumping her hand. "Why, Abe must think he's seeing a ghost every time he looks at you."

Nora smiled. "He says I remind him of his brother."

"Oh, I was thinking more of your grandmother. I swear, when I saw you coming up the drive on that old bicycle, I felt

105

like I was in a time warp—Elnora Fisher coming to pick up her eggs. Forgive me for staring. Come on inside and meet Ida."

"Before you guys go in," I requested, looking at Gramps, "I was wondering if you could tell us a little more about that lawsuit between Abe and Nora's mom."

Gramps looked uncertainly from my face to Nora's, then back to mine again. Nora, to her credit, managed to appear unsurprised. "Abe told you about it?" he asked us both.

I nodded forcefully, and Nora mirrored me.

"Abe said you would remember the details better," I added. "Since he was just a kid when it happened."

"Well, that's true," Gramps agreed. "He was only thirteen. Still recovering from his brother's death. And Paul's wife—Nora's mother—she was recovering too. Very bitter about everything, and who could blame her? But when she challenged the will, we came to Abe's defense. He would never have fought for Riverside on his own, not at his age. He wasn't a fighter. Ida and I knew that."

Nora hung on every word. Whenever he paused, she circled with her hand, asking me to urge him to continue. "So what happened with the lawsuit?" I asked.

"It was pretty nasty, I'm sorry to say. Your mother must have felt like the whole town was against her. She didn't understand how people around here felt about Elnora's boys."

"So what did you do?"

"We hired a top lawyer from Chicago and he put an airtight case together, and that was that."

"Abe won," I finished, for Nora's benefit.

"And my mom lost," Nora said.

"Then Linda ... your mother ... left town, without so much as a goodbye to any of us! We thought we'd never see you again, Nora. But here you are, all grown up and becoming a part of Riverside yourself, from what I hear. We were so very fond of that father of yours. Paul McMichael was the best science student Ida had in forty years of teaching. A born naturalist, as I'm sure your uncle has told you. And then Abe followed right in his footsteps. And looks like now you're following right along, too."

"All my life I've gotten A's in science," Nora confided to Gramps. "Even when I didn't study, I could ace my science tests."

I'd heard enough. "Why don't you take Nora inside now, Gramps?" I urged impatiently. I let them go in without me. I knew that Gram would probably burst into tears at the sight of a living, breathing girl who looked so much like her long-dead best friend. Way too much melodrama for me.

———

Two hours later, Gram insisted I drive Nora and her bike back to the cabin. Nora seemed tired and didn't object. She lifted Abe's bike into the bed of my truck, let herself in on the passenger side, and pressed her head against the back of the seat while I started the engine. "I'm *really* getting tired of everyone telling me how much I remind them of dead people," she said.

"Did she get out the old photographs?"

"*Oh* yeah. But I didn't mind. They're nice. Both of them, really nice. Why didn't they have any kids of their own?"

"I guess they tried when they were young. But it never happened. That's how Gram explained it to me. Except in more scientific terms."

While I was explaining this, Nora lifted one hip and pulled a couple of snapshots out of her back pocket. "She gave me these. One of my dad and Abe, and one of my grandmother. Who, by the way, I *do* look like. I mean *seriously*. Your gram just sat real close and stared at me. Like that made her so happy." Her voice changed, became more needling. "You don't believe I really get A's in science, do you? Are you one of those guys who think girls can't be smart in science?"

"Hey, I was raised by a woman scientist, remember? I know plenty of smart girls. I've even hooked up with a few."

She scoffed softly and then turned her gaze back to the two photographs in her hand, studying them. "Explains why she would still hate him, doesn't it? I guess it all comes down to money. My mom has been fighting with people about money her whole life. It makes me tired." She sighed and closed her eyes.

"Are you going to tell Abe you know about the lawsuit?"

"Oh ... eventually. But not tonight—I think he's still kind of shaky from my mom going off on him, don't you?"

I realized that she was asking for my opinion. The energy between us shifted slightly. But in the next breath, she said,

"Your gram told me that your mom was one of her favorite students too."

I kept my eyes on the dark road and made a mental note to give Gram hell.

"What happened to her?" Nora asked.

"I have no idea," I said. "She took off a long time ago and it's not something I think about."

"I didn't think about my dad either, until this summer," Nora said. "My mom always made it seem like he wasn't worth thinking about. Like there was nothing important to know. But your Gram doesn't do that to you, does she? That doesn't seem like something she would do."

We had turned into the cabin drive and I accelerated my truck to the front porch. "See you tomorrow," I said gruffly, prompting her to get out.

"You didn't like me mentioning your mom," she said.

"I told you … I don't think about it."

"Oh," she said. "Okay. Fine. I've certainly been *there*. So … do you want to come inside for a moment and see the moth collection?"

At this, my mouth fell open in disbelief. I managed to say, "You're kidding, right? Because that is probably the last thing in the world I want to do."

Nora's face rearranged quickly. She hopped out of the truck and slammed the door. "Never mind," she snapped. "I was thinking that maybe you were starting to be less of an asshole."

In the rearview mirror, I watched her lift her bike from

the truck bed; she swung it high with surprising ease, despite her earlier tiredness. Then she wheeled the bike to the porch without glancing back and disappeared inside.

I sat a moment in the truck, feeling wildly angry. Angry that she had brought up my mother. Angry that she always scoffed at the idea of me having girlfriends. Angry about the moths. But most of all, angry about the way she'd lifted her bike out of my truck—the arc of her narrow back, the new muscles in her bare arms and shoulders, a gracefulness that stung me. And it made me furious. I drove away, cursing at her from the safety of my truck.

——

Gramps and Gram were in the kitchen, still talking about their amazing visit from the amazing Nora. "Like seeing a ghost in my own kitchen," Gram was gushing. "A beautiful, red-headed ghost."

"What do you say we invite Abe and Nora over here for dinner some time soon?" Gramps suggested. "I'll cook ribs on the grill."

I lifted my hands slowly to get their full attention.

"Let me just make something clear on this subject, okay? Okay? I am really glad that Nora finally bothered to come over here and meet you guys. But you need to understand that her and me … we are not friends. And dealing with her everyday is not easy. In fact, some days it really sucks."

My grandparents gave each other one of their long, si- lent looks. Gram then sent Gramps a little wave, gesturing for him to leave us alone. He nodded agreeably, and got up and left the room.

As soon as we were alone, I blurted out, "What were you thinking, Gram! Bringing up my mom with Nora like that?"

"She asked me a perfectly reasonable question," Gram replied calmly. "And what I told her was incontrovertible fact. Both her father and your mother were my students, my favorite students."

"It's my private business, Gram. It's not something I want somebody like her to know!"

Gram put a hand on my shoulder, a request for me to calm down. "Well, then I misunderstood the meaning of her visit," she said. "I assumed that things were better between the two of you. The girl seemed so friendly and happy to be here."

"Oh, she's happy to be here all right. She thinks she owns Riverside and she has Abe wrapped around her little finger."

"You're still angry with her," Gram decided aloud. "Is it because she has the moths?"

This was unsettling, given the exchange Nora and I had just had. "I really don't want to talk about this tonight," I said.

"I know you're tired, son. But stay and talk with me a little longer. There's something I've been wanting to show you, ever since you first told me about finding the moth collection in Abe's basement. I've been remembering what those moths meant to Paul. How he found them and worked on them and wrote about them. In all my years of teaching,

I never had a student as passionate and single-minded about a science project as he was that year."

"You've already told me this, Gram."

"But did I tell you ... do you know ... what was happening in his life during that time?"

I remembered what Abe had told me, but kept silent.

"Let me show you something." She hurried into her little office at the back of the house and came out carrying a thick scrapbook with a hand-lettered title: *Buchanan High School*. She thumped it onto the kitchen table, opened it, and leaned close, flipping the plastic pages until she came to a newspaper clipping from the *Niles Gazette*. The article included a grainy photograph—a boy around my own age holding a moth case at his waist. *Buchanan High School Student Wins State Science Honors,* the headline read. Underneath the photo were the words, *First-Place Winner Says His Dream is to Build His Own Nature Center."*

"His mother died two months later, Peter." Gram looked at me. "Then he was offered a full scholarship to Michigan State, but he wouldn't leave Buchanan because he couldn't leave his brother. There was no bitterness in his decision. He loved Riverside so much."

"Is this supposed to be making me feel better?"

"Paul McMichael was the same age you are when he started collecting moths," she continued. "He put aside everything else in his life—friends, girlfriends, other interests, other needs. He was searching for something."

"I need to sleep," I said.

"What are you searching for?" she asked.

"Good night, Gram." I lurched to my room.

"Where are all your friends this summer?" she called, but I didn't answer.

———

That night I dreamt that one of the moths escaped Nora's room and found its way back to the basement of the Visitor's Center; I found it sitting on my workbench. It was a species that I'd never seen before—huge and fur-covered and the size of a small owl, with beautiful blue and green markings on its wings. When it flew up, the wings made a soft, flapping sound, like the shaking of a pillow, around my head. I was deliriously happy that it had come back to me. It landed again and sat a moment, watching me and fluttering its great wings. I approached it, realizing that it had a human child's face. Its antennae were criss-crossed with cobwebs, as though it had been hiding somewhere dusty. *Were you part of the collection?* I asked.

Nobody ever caught me, she replied.

I reached for the window behind her, to free her, and pushed it open. But instead of flying out the window, she perched on my outstretched arm like a huge parrot. The soft fur of her wings brushed against the side of my face before she flew away.

Moth Journal

Paul McMichael

Buchanan, Michigan

October 1988

Every small and insignificant moth is born with everything it needs to build an actual house around itself. Inside this safe house, the moth transforms in secret. First the larvae, or caterpillar, chooses a suitable stem to attach itself to, then it spins a cocoon, an actual chamber that is at first soft but then becomes hard, like a shell, so as to better protect and hide its inhabitant.

The larvae then transforms into a damp, crumpled creature, splitting the case when the metamorphosis is complete. The moth awakens, unfolds, dries out its wings and flies away, into the rest of its life, leaving behind the tattered remains of a room spun from its own being.

Spun from its own being! How can such a miracle be possible? How can any creature create a room from its own being? And why do these facts fill me with happiness, as though I am the first person to discover them?

Tonight, for the last time this year, I will take my new truck and my new recipe for moth bait to the clearing between the pond and the river and if luck is with me, I will find and capture a late-flying Cecropia or a Polyphemus or, if I am really lucky, a Luna. I'll head early to the lab in the morning to show off my captives and share with Mrs. Shelton my fool-proof method, tested and perfected in the swamps of her own property—the valleys and prairie and swamps of Riverside, where moths are safe to fly and breed and hide in the birch and maple trees on my river.

8. Pinned

I overslept, arrived late to Riverside, and found Nora and Christina in the kitchen drinking coffee with their shoulders close, giggling at some private joke. Nora had lately become very chummy with Christina, the two of them always talking and whispering and often working side by side. It didn't seem to bother Bella; maybe she liked having someone else occupy her mom's attention. But it bugged the hell out of me.

"Where's Bella?" I asked them gruffly. They looked up at me and Christina pointed out the kitchen window, toward the lodge. "She's fox-sitting and waiting for her hero. Guess I'd better get to my work before the big boss man fires me." And she strutted out of the kitchen, singing a few lines from an old blues song, "Big Boss Man."

Nora lingered as I poured and stirred my coffee. "Can I talk to you for just a minute?" she asked.

I kept my back to her, and she added, "I know, I know—I'm the last person in the world you want to talk to. But this time it's about Christina."

"Afraid I've got a pretty busy morning."

"Oh you do *not*. God, you're always acting like everything you do is so much more important than what anybody else does. It's about *Christina*. I *know* you like her. I know you appreciate her. And for your information, Christina and my dad went to the same high school. She actually *remembers* him."

Deep sigh of boredom.

"Look, I just need you to explain to me what the deal is between Christina and Abe."

"I have no idea what you're talking about."

"Come on—you *must* have noticed. I mean, does Abe *like* Christina? Does he have any *feelings* towards her?"

I have to admit, I'd been wondering this very thing myself ever since Christina and Bella came back from their vacation. I knew that Abe genuinely enjoyed having Christina around, but I didn't know what she meant to him, not really. Still, I was not about to enter into a discussion about it with Nora. "I have work to do," I reminded her, turning to leave the room.

"She's *crazy* about him," Nora persisted. "Have you noticed how she stares at the back of his head all the time? And how she's always quoting something he said? Does Bella know? Has she ever mentioned it to you?"

"Bella's noticed," I admitted.

"Is Abe just completely unaware?"

I shook my head. "He's hopeless about women. Just really, really shy."

"How did he get that way? My dad wasn't shy. Christina said he had lots of girlfriends. Lots of girls had crushes on him. But Abe—I mean—do you think he's *ever* had a girlfriend?"

"Never," I reported.

"Don't you think we should try to help him?"

"Help him what?"

"I don't know—get over his shyness. Get closer to Christina. So that he won't be so all alone?"

This made me feel defensive. "He's not all alone."

She rolled her eyes at me. "Oh, come on, Shelton! He lives by himself in a cabin in the woods and the only place he ever goes is to this office here. He's almost thirty years old and he doesn't have any friends except you, and he's *never* had a girlfriend. That's *alone*. Get a clue."

I scowled.

"Oh, I know, I know," she added. "You and Abe go *way* back. But don't tell me you're never planning to leave this place. Like you won't ever go to college or live anyplace else or have a girlfriend yourself. And it's not like your grandparents are going to live forever, either. Wake up. They're *old*."

"Jeez," I protested. "Be a little negative, why don't you?"

She was turning to leave, but before she disappeared I

threw out one last defense, "Maybe it's not so bad, being a loner."

"You would know," she said, without turning around.

"Yeah, well, you would know too."

Then she did turn around. "Okay, so we're both loners. So we know what that's like. But Abe isn't a loner. He's *alone*. There's a difference."

She left me scowling over my coffee. The last word again.

———

For the next couple of days, I found myself paying more attention to the way Abe acted around Christina, testing my theory that Abe really *did* like Christina, more than was obvious to the untrained eye. He no longer avoided the Visitor's Center on the days that she came in. He let her constantly rearrange the kitchen without complaining. He put up with her occasional teasing, even though it obviously embarrassed him. He'd even started calling her by her first name, pronouncing it strangely with an accent on the final "a," like it was a difficult name for him to get his mouth around. Sometimes when she wasn't around, he would speculate aloud about what he might ask her to do the next time she came in. It wasn't much, but it was a lot for Abe.

So, while he and I were surveying the prairie, I carefully brought up the subject. "Abe, do you remember how at first you said you didn't want any volunteers at Riverside?"

He lifted his binoculars to his eyes. "I remember."

"Who would have ever thought we'd find somebody as

great as Christina, right? Somebody who cares about this place just as much as we do."

I waited for his reaction, but he kept silent, scanning the prairie.

"Abe?"

Still scanning, he asked, "Have you been talking to Nora about this?"

"About what?"

"Christina."

"Well ... maybe she said *something* ... I was just making a comment about—"

Abe cut me off. "Nora has decided that I don't like being alone. But I think you know me better than that, Pete." He lowered the binoculars. "I'm glad that Christina is part of the team. Bella too. And you're right, they do care about this place. It's been good having them here. We're all very lucky this summer."

Lucky. I was momentarily taken aback by his choice of words. *Lucky* was the last word I would have used to describe how I felt that summer, but I liked hearing him say it. I also liked hearing him say that I knew him better than Nora. In fact, the pleasure of this compliment settled over me as I strode through the prairie grass beside him. Man to man, we chose a perfect future site for an observation deck—in complete agreement as usual. Then we drove back to the Center in a comfortable silence. All was well between us. I knew him best. Being a loner was fine, noble even. Nora was wrong. I knew better. Abe and I were lucky.

———

"Did you ask him?" Nora whispered. It had been a long, hot day; I was in the office, tallying up bills for installing the windows in the lodge, and I was tired.

"Drop it," I said. "Don't bug Abe and don't encourage Christina."

Nora scowled. "I will not *drop* it. Just because you can't be bothered to think about it."

"I did think about it. I even asked Abe about it and he said he's fine with things the way they are."

She was exasperated. "Well, of course, he would say that to *you!*"

"Look, is there something else you want to talk about? Because we're finished with this subject."

Big mistake to invite her to choose a new subject. She paused and tipped her head, her expression suddenly challenging. "We could talk about moths," she said.

"We are not talking about moths."

"Did I mention that I painted my bedroom? I painted the walls and the ceiling dark blue, so they would look like a night sky, and then ... "

"Nora, I don't care."

" ... I hung the moth cases in two rows, one on each wall, right about shoulder-high ... "

I was suddenly angry again. I slammed down my pen and glared at her, warningly.

She wasn't fazed. "Do you know why Abe is so weird

about those moths?" she asked in a rush. "He didn't even want me to hang them on the walls."

"Are you deaf? I said I don't care!"

"You do so care."

"Jesus, would you just leave me alone? I'm through talking to you! Get out of here!"

"Grudge-holder," she hissed, exiting. Christina entered the next moment, wearing a paint-spattered bandana over her hair and a *now-what-have-you-done* expression on her face.

"Don't give me that look, Christina. You don't know how hard it is, having her in my face every day."

"Oh, come on—are you two fighting about those moths again?"

"We are not *fighting* about the moths. She wanted them, she got them, and that's the end of it."

"She feels guilty, Pete. She knows they were important to you. Maybe if you two could just sit down and have a little heart-to-heart—"

"Christina, I don't care! If Nora wants to put them in her bed and sleep with them, I don't care!"

"She *sleeps* with them?" Christina repeated, aghast.

I covered my face. "No, she doesn't actually *sleep* with them! She hung the cases on the walls of the pantry."

"She sleeps in a *pantry*?"

"It used to be a pantry. Abe made it into a bedroom."

"So you're saying she hung her father's moth collection

on the walls of her bedroom? Oh, Pete! That's so beautiful. Isn't that just too beautiful to bear?"

I got up and left the room, needing air.

———

Again, I had the feeling of being a trespasser—not so much unwelcome as disconnected to the cabin now, clearly on the outside. But I entered. I moved quickly through the rooms, through the empty kitchen. The door of the pantry was slightly ajar; I pushed it open and let a slight breeze move through the tunnel of Nora's room. The space held her fragrance—her shampoo and her laundry and her perfume. On the table at the head of her bed were two cheaply framed photographs—one of Elnora standing in front of a barn, and one showing two bare-chested, curly-headed boys in a canoe. The smaller of these boys was a miniature Abe, waving at the camera with an open hand. The other boy was older and taller, manning the oars with a somber, knowing smile.

I looked at the walls. Nora had painted them a dark, cobalt blue and mounted the wooden moth cases on either side of her bed in two shoulder-high rows, leading in parallel lines to her little window. Five on one side, six on the other—all but the broken *Cecropia*. I had to admit, it was a dramatic sight. My heart ached. I stood a long moment, feeling something unfamiliar, a kind of longing I didn't fully understand.

I ducked my head at the doorway while passing through, and as I emerged back into the kitchen, I saw that someone was standing at the sink. It startled me so thoroughly that for a moment the room spun around my head. I closed my eyes tightly, then opened them—and saw that it was Nora.

"If you don't care, then why are you here?" she asked.

Her eyes were the brightest blue I'd ever seen. What could I say? There was nothing to say. She'd followed me on her bicycle and caught me trespassing, invading her bedroom—and perhaps worst of all, caring enough about what she'd done with the moths to do all these things. I had no defense. I stood, silent as a muzzled dog, and waited for whatever her reaction would be. She took several steps toward me, and it occurred to me that she might slap me—which I would have also had to endure—and I tightened my jaw and shoulders in anticipation. But to my complete surprise, she instead grabbed one of my useless hands, tugged at it, and led me back into the pantry.

"This is the first room of my own I've ever had," she said. "When Abe first put that window in, I was so mad that I wouldn't even speak to him. I had even started packing, pretending I had somewhere else to go. But Abe wanted to make it right again between us, so he went back to Riverside and got the window. And when he came back he asked me to help him install it. And I did, I helped him, even though I still wasn't speaking to him—we did it in complete silence. When we were finished, he told me that all the McMichaels were good carpenters and that I was a good carpenter too. Me. Who had never picked up a hammer in my life. But I still kept acting like I didn't care.

"And for a few days after that, every time he asked me if

I was happy about the window, I told him I didn't care. For a whole week I said I didn't care. He'd given me my own room and put a window in it for me. Nobody's ever done anything like that for me before. It was … unbearable. So I said I didn't care. Because it was painful—how much I cared."

Her eyes were killing me. I needed to look past them, and away from her face and her mouth, to the moths. My eyes settled on the emerald green *Luna*, the moth nearest the open window, and I focused hard on it and took a few deep breaths, trying to find a way out of my confusion and embarrassment. When I turned my eyes back to her face, I saw that the sunlight from the window was backlighting her, shadowing her eyes, accenting her lower lip. She looked so beautiful. And it was scary to suddenly be seeing her as beautiful. I think she sensed my fear, because her face grew softer.

"You do that too," she said. "You say you don't care."

I shook my head. "I don't even know you."

"Yes, you do. You know me. I'm like you."

I stopped shaking my head, stopped refusing to accept what she was saying. I let my body fill with relief. And longing—both at once. Slowly I put a hand on each of her shoulders and pulled her against me. She didn't resist; she came to me easily and let me hold her tightly. I clung to her for a moment and then instinctively pulled my head away from her shoulder and leaned in.

In that narrow room, standing in a square of light from her window and surrounded by moths, I kissed Nora. Our arms came around each other somehow and we were joined from head to toe, as if we were in a display case ourselves, pinned to each other and to our kiss. It was a long moment, but it passed finally, and I released her at the same moment she released me.

The end of our kiss was a mutual gasp. I looked around myself one more time and then I bolted. I rushed from the bedroom, the kitchen, the cabin, the driveway, fumbling back into my truck and heading back to Riverside, still feeling her mouth against mine and thinking, *what just happened?*

Moth Journal

Paul McMichael

Buchanan, Michigan

The Paul McMichael foolproof method for baiting
moths at Riverside, perfected in October 1988:

Supplies needed: containers for specimens, butterfly
net, jar of sugar bait, paint brush, ultraviolet light
(Mrs. Shelton has one), folding stool, repellent, mosquito guard for head, food, blanket, flashlight and
notebook.

1) Choose a cloudy night with moonlight, new
    moon, if possible. Light drizzle is best or, even
    better, a night when rain is coming. Early fall
    is ideal for collecting, but if it is a warm fall,
    moths will be on the move until October.

2) Find a clearing not far from river or pond—at edge of the woods is best, or some kind of open space with trees around.

3) Hang a thin white sheet between two trees and put a mobile light source behind it, ultraviolet is best.

4) Paint tree trunks with sugaring mixture. My sugar bait is a boiled and cooled combination of sugar water, honey, molasses, spoiled fruit and beer—this must be thick enough to stick to the bark and not run off.

5) Wait for dark. Wait for moths: blanket on ground, stool on blanket, leaning against a tree is good. Apply repellent and mosquito guard as needed.

6) Catch moths with net or jars, depending on location. Avoid shining flashlight unnecessarily; this will disorient and cause moths to escape. Put flashlight at low beam at base of

tree and slowly move up. Once several moths
are caught, put in containers with Glanz fluid
so as to preserve as quickly as possible.

This is how I caught my first Cecropia.

9. Driver's Seat

Nora did not come back to Riverside that day. Abe asked me several times if I had seen her. Finally, feeling cornered, I told him that I thought she might have gone back to the cabin. "The cabin?" he repeated, puzzled. "She never said she was going to the cabin. Did she tell you that?"

I looked away, my color rising. "No, I just thought maybe...because she's not...you know...here."

"She promised she would finish painting that lattice today," Abe remembered, scratching his head. "And now Christina's gone, too."

He picked up the office phone and dialed his own number. "Hey, we were just wondering where you are!" he exclaimed. A pause, and then he asked, "What do you mean?"

I ducked my head at my desk, appalled that Nora might

be telling Abe what had happened at the cabin. "You take it easy, then," Abe said mildly, then hung up and turned to me. "You were right, Pete. She said she's going to bed. Hope she's not coming down with something."

"Hope not," I seconded weakly.

Abe was watching me now, faintly concerned. "You feeling okay yourself?" he asked. "You look a little flushed."

"I'm just hot," I said. "It's hot in here, all of sudden." I got up and turned on the office fan, fiddling with the speeds, keeping my back to Abe for several minutes to hide my disorientation.

———

That night I was sitting up on my bed with a birders magazine, trying not to think about Nora, when Gram knocked gently on my half-opened door and then settled herself into the leather chair beside my bed. "Didn't you tell me recently that Nora wants anything that ever belonged to her father?"

I nodded, wary.

"Well, I've been wondering ... I'm wondering how much you know about that truck you've been driving for the past year."

"It was Gramps' truck," I said. "What else is there to know about it?"

"Abe has never said anything about it?"

"What would Abe have to say about it?"

"Listen to me. Conrad did in fact drive the truck for many years before giving it to you. But years before that, Abe gave the truck to him. It was a kind of payment for Conrad's help during the trial. And Abe had no interest in owning it himself. For several reasons, not the least of which was that he was too young to drive at the time."

As she spoke, a warning light went off in my head. "Gram, how did Abe get a truck?"

"It originally belonged to Paul."

"Wait just a minute, Gram. Are you telling me that I'm driving a truck that once belonged to Paul McMichael?"

"I'm afraid that's not all. It's the same truck Paul was driving the night he died."

More lights, more alarms. I covered my face. "Gram, please don't tell me this. This is just way too weird for me!"

She patted my arm so I would calm down. "He didn't actually die in the truck, Peter. He was thrown from the cab. It was the most improbable accident—an ice storm … and the truck spun out on a patch of black ice and Paul was thrown from behind the wheel and flew head-first into a tree. Killed instantly. Instantly! The truck ended up on its side in a snow-filled ditch, with barely a scratch on it."

Gram's face was controlled as she was relaying this, but I could tell it was really difficult for her even to talk about it. Her pale blue eyes had gone unnaturally wide and her voice had dropped almost to a whisper. "It was so … *unlikely*, Peter! So *momentary!* That remarkable young man with so much to live for—gone in an instant. Oh, it broke all our hearts for the longest time." She closed her eyes.

"Why hasn't anybody told me this before now?" I groaned.

"I never expected it to come up, Peter. Nor did Conrad. And Abe has very likely forgotten all about it. He was determined to leave his past behind. He never spoke about that time in his life and he didn't ... keep things. That's why I was so surprised when you told me he still had the moths. He was anxious to give Conrad the truck. We never discussed it with him after that. But in case it ever did come up, Peter, if Nora were to discover ... I think it would be better if she heard about the history of the truck from you."

"But if nobody knows but you and Gramps and Abe," I insisted, "who would tell her?"

"Well ... something occurred to me today. If Nora ran away from home, as you suggested ... and if her mother did come to Buchanan looking for her—Linda, if she came to Buchanan—*she* would remember that it was Paul's truck."

"Abe says she won't come here, Gram."

"Does he? That may be wishful thinking on his part. Maybe the best thing now is for all of us, including Abe, to be ready."

I was shaking my head. "I can't just tell Nora that I'm driving around in her dead father's truck—she'll go psycho on me all over again!"

"Oh, I don't think so," Gram disagreed. "The girl I met seems to have moved far beyond going psycho on you. Although you might have to brace yourself for some of those dreaded female tears."

I grimaced, unnerved at the thought, and then another distressing possibility hit me. "Oh, *man*! What if she wants me to give the truck back, too?"

"What if she does? You can always get another truck. But you can't keep this information from the girl for your own convenience. This is something she would prefer to know, I'm sure of it. And I'm sure that you can think of a way to tell her. You're a smart person. Do it carefully. Take her out for an ice cream."

I was about to scoff at this old-fashioned idea, but then I caught her eye—and saw that Gram was teasing me. She knew very well that what she was suggesting was more complicated than an ice-cream date.

"I didn't want to know any of this, Gram."

She nodded sadly. "I wish it weren't necessary for you to know. I wish Nora's father hadn't ever died. I wish many things had been otherwise, including some that concern you. But you really do need to tell Nora about the truck. It seems somehow cruel not to."

Cruel, I thought, contemplating the word as Gram left the room. *Wouldn't want to do anything cruel, would we? No matter what someone long ago did to me.*

———

The morning after the kiss, Nora came into the office behind Abe, seeming almost shy; she wouldn't meet my eyes. I felt equally embarrassed. And also responsible. I stayed behind my desk, hunching over my sketchpad, wondering what to do. When Abe had left us alone, I made a clumsy effort to reassure her. "You don't have to feel weird about yesterday. I don't know what got into me. I'm sorry. I was just … really confused."

"Confused?" she repeated. She drew back, clearly unhappy with my statement. *"Confused?"*

She was almost out the door when I called out, "Nora, I'm just trying to say that we can move on if—"

"Oh, I'm moving on," she assured me. She snapped her fingers. "Moved on. Never happened."

Later that morning, I saw from the office window that she was weeding the terrace garden. I decided to try again. When she saw me coming toward her, she stood up and crossed her arms and scowled. I searched my mind for something to quickly say that wouldn't make things worse. I came up with this: "Heard anything from your mom lately?"

Her expression turned suspicious. "How did you know I heard from my mom?"

"I didn't know. I just … I was just asking."

She hesitated, deciding whether or not to continue, then said, "She called yesterday, actually. Right after you left the cabin. You know. Right after you got so … *confused.*"

"Look, when I said that, I just meant—"

Nora shook her head, refusing further explanation. "She wanted to talk to Abe again, but I wouldn't let her. I explained that he wasn't home—I didn't want her upsetting him, anyway. She said she can tell that people are turning me against her. And that she wouldn't stand for it. She said it in this kind of threatening way. And then I got this feeling… this feeling like… like maybe my mom will try to do something to Abe. Something that would hurt him. For letting me stay with him."

"What could she possibly do?" I asked.

"I don't know," Nora replied. "But I think she hurt him pretty bad when he was thirteen. With the lawsuit and everything. I was even thinking maybe it's the reason he's so scared of women."

As she was speaking I noticed her hands—she was biting her nails again, and her thumbs especially looked red and sore. She saw me noticing this, clenched her hands, and looked away, upset.

A pause. "Do you want to take a drive somewhere, Nora? Get your mind off this?"

"I don't know," she muttered.

"Come on. You and me, let's get some lunch."

Her eyes went round and bright. "Oh my god. Do you think we could maybe get a hamburger somewhere?"

"We can get anything you want."

"I haven't had a real burger since I got here, Pete," she said. "I'd kill for a burger and fries right now. Make it two." Then she laughed at herself and I found myself laughing too. She had an odd, husky laugh, like a person who laughs rarely. Had I ever heard the sound before? Suddenly, I wanted to wrap my arms around her again, keep the laughter between us a moment longer. But instead I jerked my thumb toward the parking lot and we started walking toward my truck, Nora complaining the whole way about the fact that Abe was a vegetarian. But when we were next to my truck, she surprised me by asking, "Can I drive?"

There was something challenging in her voice and I met her eyes uneasily, wondering if she knew something. "Why do you want to drive?"

"Why not? Unless you're one of those guys who can't stand to let a girl get behind the wheel."

"I'm not one of those guys" I insisted. "But just let me drive today, okay?"

"You *are*! You're one of those guys!"

"You don't know what you're talking about," I barked, losing patience. "Do you want to get a burger or not?"

This made her climb in obediently, but she was smiling, pleased with herself for pissing me off. When the truck was moving, she said, "I can't drive, actually. I lost my license back in Indianapolis. I was driving by myself on my temporary."

"How'd you get around after that?"

"Somebody drove me," she said. She added softly, "Don't ask."

———

I took her to a Buchanan landmark, the Olde Village Inn, where the menu is written out on two huge dry-erase boards behind the bar. The Inn itself is a kind of tunnel with a single row of black Formica tables, red vinyl chairs, and wood paneling everywhere. Flags from different countries hang from the ceiling. Nora looked up at them and grinned approvingly. "Great place," she said. "Reminds me of some of the roadside diners in the U.P."

"When were you up there?"

"Way long ago. With my mom. We used to go on road trips, just the two of us. Before Steve."

"Steve is your stepdad?"

"I don't call him my stepdad."

"But that's what he is."

She scowled.

"Why do I get the feeling you don't like him?"

She pressed her lips together, which I took as a signal that this subject was off-limits. I let it drop. We ordered cheeseburgers and fries. The food, as usual, was great. Nora ate like a starving person, smiling blissfully after each bite. I felt both of us relaxing and I took a chance.

"So, who drove you around after you lost your license?"

"You don't want to know," she insisted.

"Yes, I do."

"Why?" she asked. "So you can feel superior?"

This surprised me. "No! I just … I don't know anything about the situation you came from."

"I came from hell," she said. But then she smirked at herself, for how melodramatic that sounded.

"Could you be a little more specific?"

Her tone was impatient. "Okay, the person who was driving me around was my boss at work. I worked at a pizza place and he had a big crush on me."

"So if he was your boss, then he ... "

"Was way older than me, right. But I let him drive me around. I know. It sounds pathetic. I finally had to quit. But if you tell Abe—"

"I'm not going to tell Abe!"

She shook her head. "My life was such a complete mess back then. I did so many stupid things. But I'm not like that now. I'm not that crazy girl anymore. And I swear, I'm not going to end up like my mom, married to somebody I can't trust. No way."

Then, as though to forcefully change the subject, she said, "As soon as Bella goes to Chicago, I'm going to talk Uncle Abe into inviting Christina over for dinner."

"Bella's going to Chicago?"

"Christina told me that Bella spends every August with her dad. I guess he's a jazz musician in Chicago or something cool like that. He teaches at a music school. Christina says she gets really lonely when Bella leaves. I figure August would be a perfect time for Abe to make his move."

"Nora—really, you should just forget this whole Christina-Abe thing. I know him. He'll never do it."

"Oh yes, he will—he'll do it if I ask him. He'll do anything I ask him to do."

This rubbed me the wrong way. "Nora, come on. Getting Abe to start something with Christina is not the same as getting him to buy you stuff."

She stopped in mid-bite, lowering her mangled sandwich to her plate and narrowed her eyes, insulted. "What's that supposed to mean?" she asked. When I didn't answer, she pressed, "Do you still think all I want is for Abe to buy me stuff? Like, that's why I'm here?"

I looked down at my own plate, fearing I'd just ruined our lunch.

"Answer me, Pete! You still think I'm using Abe?"

I admitted, a little defensively, "I don't know what I think about you."

Her anger was rising. "Why would you want to even sit here with me if that's what you think?"

"Nora, I don't want to fight."

"Oh no, you don't want to *fight*. You just want to be able to tell me I don't care about Abe and I'll just sit here and agree with you!"

"Hey look, you're always making these pronouncements about what kind of guy I am. Like I have no life outside of Riverside, like I'm a loner, like I'm the kind of guy who won't let a girl drive my truck, or I'm blind about stuff. Why is it okay for you to do that to me, but if I question you at all—"

"Because we're different, okay? You grew up here. You *belong* here. Your grandparents are nice. Everybody treats you like you're wonderful—like you're the damn *prince* of Riverside. You have no idea what it's like to come from where I come from. But I told you, I'm really trying to change. And I don't like you assuming that I still don't appreciate Abe, just because it took me a while to understand what he was trying to give me."

I put up my hands in surrender. I felt discouraged, unsure of whether or not we would ever be able to talk without arguing. We finished our lunch in silence. But on the way back to the truck, Nora surprised me by taking hold of one of my arms and tugging on it, to make me stop walking and look at her. "People change," she said. "*You* did."

"How did I change?"

"A few weeks ago, you hated me. Now you're just *confused* about me."

I had to smile. We were both smiling. A long, promising moment, so promising that I impulsively angled in for a kiss, but Nora pulled back, let go of my arm and slipped away, jumping into her side of the truck.

"So when are you going to show me how to drive this heap?" she asked as I started the engine. "I've never driven a stick. It looks fun. We can stay on the back roads where nobody will see us."

Again I remembered what Gram had asked me to do, but couldn't find the words in that moment. I met her eyes, struggling. "Maybe I'm not the best person to teach you things," I said, thinking of our earlier disasters.

"No, I promise I'll listen. I'll let you be the official know-it-all of driving a truck."

I laughed weakly and felt doomed. All during the ride back to Riverside I wondered when, and on what back road, I would find the courage to tell her whose truck we were driving and why it was mine. Beside me, Nora fiddled with the radio dials and found a station playing Creedence—"Green River," a perfect song to vent my frustration on. I sang along in my worst gravelly voice until Nora held her ears.

Moth Journal

Paul McMichael

Buchanan, Michigan

October 1988

The black and orange Pyrrharctia Isabella is a hardy little moth that begins as a wooly caterpillar which, according to Mrs. Shelton, the local farmers once believed could actually predict the weather! They would check out the ratio of orange to black on the caterpillar's body and predict from this how hard and long the winter would be. Mrs. Shelton told me that her own father used to actually check out the caterpillars in November and schedule his plantings by their color. Imagine one insignificant insect creature holding such crucial information for the farmers!

I can relate to this completely because I have this feeling that the moths I have collected hold some sort of information for me. Something about life and death and what is beautiful and what is unexplainable and what is coming. I want to capture this mystery and control it and use it and <u>preserve</u> it, not like a farmer but like a scientist. In spite of everything that has been happening to me, I have never been so happy!

10. Back Roads

"What are you doing here?" Nora called from Abe's porch. I'd been idling in her driveway, waiting for her to hear my noisy muffler and come outside. From this distance it was not possible to read her face, to know if she was happy or unhappy to see me.

"You feel like getting an ice cream?" I asked. It was Saturday night, kind of late, but I had spent the last few hours procrastinating and hit the road to the cabin later than I'd intended. "Come on. I'll take you into a great place in Niles."

"Uncle Abe?" she called over her shoulder. "Me and Pete are just going to drive over to Niles for an ice cream, okay?"

Abe came to the door. He stood behind Nora a moment, then moved past her, walking by himself right up to my side of the truck. His expression was so gruff and bewildered that

I had to fight not to laugh. "You're going all the way to Niles just for ice cream?" he asked, like the idea was completely insane.

"Abe, it's no big deal," I insisted. "I just thought I'd get the girl out of the house on a Saturday night."

He scowled. "How long?"

"Maybe a couple of hours?"

"Back before dark?"

"Geez, Abe, it'll be dark in like half an hour! Would you relax? I'm just making an effort to get along better with Nora. We'll be back before you know it."

Nora had gone to get her purse; now she came up behind Abe, patting his broad back before climbing into the truck. "It's *okay*, Uncle Abe. I promise I won't hurt him."

We left him standing in the drive, dumbfounded to see the two of us driving off together.

———

Niles is bigger than Buchanan. The St. Joseph River cuts through the center of town more dramatically; there are park benches along the rapids and boardwalks curving through the downtown. We parked the truck and made our way down to the boardwalk as the sun was setting. I settled onto a bench at the river and gestured for Nora to sit beside me. She did, but she was jiggling her legs impatiently. "Where's this ice cream place?" she asked. "I need something big and full of chocolate right now."

"Okay, but first there's something I need to tell you."

"Can't we walk while you talk?" Nora asked, getting up.

I pulled her by the hand back to the bench. "Just sit for a minute more and listen, okay, Nora? It's … about my truck. I've been trying to figure out the right way to tell you something kind of important about my truck."

"Oh, I know what you're going to say," she said, amused. "You don't want me to drive it."

"It's not the driving thing. It's more about … the actual truck."

Nora wrinkled her forehead at my seriousness. "What is *up* with you tonight?" she asked. She stood up again. "Come on. Let's walk."

But I didn't get up and she sat back down reluctantly, making an effort to be patient with me.

"Abe gave the truck to Gramps a long time ago, Nora. Right around the time when you were born."

"That doesn't make sense, Pete. Why would Abe have his own truck before he was old enough to drive?"

"Because it was your dad's truck before it was Abe's."

The wrinkles in Nora's forehead deepened. "This truck? The one you're driving *now*?"

"I didn't know, Nora. Gram told me about it last week, and we didn't want you to find out some other—"

"Pete," Nora interrupted. "Pete, my dad was killed in a car accident."

"Right," I said miserably.

"So does this truck … does this … your truck … have something to do with that accident?"

I was almost whispering. "I swear I didn't know until a week ago, Nora."

"Okay! OKAY! OKAY!!! I've been riding around all summer in the truck my dad *died* in?"

I reached out to put an arm around her, but she shoved my arm away. "He didn't actually die in the truck, Nora," I insisted pleadingly. "He was thrown out of it when it skidded on the ice, and he went headfirst into a tree."

Nora covered her ears. "Shut up!" she cried. "Just shut up! God, do you have any idea how this is for me? Hearing the details of how my dad died from *you*? Oh God, this is too weird!"

"It's weird for me, too. I'm sorry, Nora."

"And you're not even related to me! You didn't even know me until a month ago!"

"Look, I had to tell you, okay? I couldn't keep it a secret once I knew!"

She turned to me then, uncovered her ears, and looked about to cry. "Secrets are easier, Pete. Secrets are what I'm used to."

"But I don't want it to be like that with us." Then, because I was afraid she would cry, I asked pleadingly, "Do you still want an ice cream?"

She closed her eyes tightly and held her head. "Oh my God, I don't think I can get back into that truck again."

"Okay, we'll walk. It's just up the hill and around the corner. Come on. Walk with me."

To my relief, she stood up and we began to walk. I put

my arm around her waist and this time she didn't push me away. I bought her a double-chocolate ice cream cone, and one for myself, and then we walked back to the river. When we were settled again on the bench, I asked her if she wanted the truck.

When it dawned on her what I was offering, she put a hand on my arm. "Oh Pete. Did you think I would take your truck away too?"

"I didn't know."

"No, I don't want it, Pete. And I don't want to learn to drive it either. That would be way too morbid, even for me."

We finished our cones. I took her hand, and we walked along the river on the boardwalk for a little while, watching the sun set. We moved in the darkening light and talked some more, and were silent some more, like friends. More than friends. When we finally left Niles, she was brave about getting into the truck and I was proud of her, and grateful that the truck was still mine. We drove past the old stone train station, the place where she'd first arrived, and I asked her something I'd been wondering since way back in early June. "What would you have done that night, if Abe had refused to come and get you?"

"I don't know," she admitted. "It's not like I had a plan B. But he was there in like twenty minutes—I think he must have driven about a hundred miles an hour."

"He was pretty unglued."

"Oh, I know," she agreed. "I was too. Still am, actually. I can't believe I even have an uncle like Abe."

We pulled up to the cabin and I could see Abe's shadowy image through the living room window. We saw him jump up from the sofa and come to the front door. The porch light was on; he stood under it, and we could see that he was angry. "You said you'd be right back," he accused us.

"We got to talking, Uncle Abe," Nora explained, jumping out of the truck. "I guess we lost track of time."

To our surprise, he turned his back on us and stormed back into the cabin. "Whoa, he's really mad!" Nora said, dismayed.

"Let's go in and talk to him."

"No, I'll go," she insisted. "You just wait right here a minute. Please?"

Before I could protest, she rushed inside. Through the living room window I could see the two of them talking— Abe with head lowered and arms crossed tightly across his chest; Nora pleading and gesturing with her hands. After a few minutes, she came back out to the truck. "He was afraid something had happened to us," she reported sadly.

"Should I come in and apologize?"

"Not now. You'd better just go home, okay?"

It wasn't really a question. I started the engine. "Will I see you tomorrow?" I asked.

"I don't know," she said. "Let's just … let's just see."

She was backing away from me as she spoke. "Thanks for telling me about the truck," she called softly.

I shrugged, hiding how stung I felt that she was sending me away, not only from her, but also from Abe. But neither of these disappointments compared to my biggest one—that I would not be kissing her that night.

Abe had come out of the house; he was standing on the porch again, hovering as I eased out of his driveway. In my rearview mirror, I saw that Nora was watching me from where she stood in the middle of the drive, her face in shadows.

Moth Journal

Paul McMichael

Buchanan, Michigan

November 1988

The female *Automeris Io*, of the family *Saturnidae*, has the most amazing eyespots of all the moths I've collected—they are so startling and so piercing when the moth's' yellow wings are open, like black-rimmed eyes. The whole idea that moths have these incredible markings that are hidden when it is at rest, but then just explode into sight if the moth takes flight or is threatened by an enemy (a bird or another insect), and suddenly there is this facelike image that is meant to confuse or scare away enemies—it is so astounding! And even many of the small, plain moths have a version of an eyespot, or a distorted eyespot—an eyespot substitute. What other insect, or other animal in all of nature, has markings that intentionally create a small, wide-eyed face, staring out at its enemies and making them unsure of who and what they are seeing!

I am working almost entirely now at the lab after school. Mrs. Shelton has given me my own Meade Binocular Microscope, and every few days she leaves a new book or article. Yesterday she asked me why Cathy never comes to the lab anymore, and I told her that we broke up. When she asked why, I told her that Cathy is the sort of girl who prefers butterflies to moths. Mrs. Shelton thought this was pretty funny—she understood. When I am finished with moths, I told her, I'll get back to girls.

When you are finished with moths, Mrs. Shelton said, beware of girls who want to collect you.

11. Canoes

All the next day—a Sunday—I tried to reach her. She wasn't answering her cell and there was no answer at the cabin. In the mid-afternoon, I drove to Riverside, hoping to find one or both of them there. I'd rehearsed an apology for Abe and fantasized about arranging the moment when I would be alone again with Nora.

When I saw Abe's jeep in the Riverside parking lot, and heard Thor barking happily from the porch, I was ecstatic. But the office was empty. I wandered out to the gardens and checked the lodge, but found no one. Next I headed down the Ridge Trail to the river. My best hope was to find Nora alone, but I fully expected to find her and Abe together at Elnora's Point, where I would join them and make my peace with Abe.

Elnora's Point was deserted too, although when I looked around, I saw fresh boot prints to the riverbank and a muddy bowl where the old canoe usually sat. The canoe was gone! Abe and Nora were out on the river! My heart constricted painfully. I scanned the horizon for the familiar silver gleam of the canoe and realized, after a few moments of staring at the water, that what I was feeling was jealousy. Not a new emotion that summer, but this time I wasn't feeling jealous of Nora and her connection to Abe—I was feeling jealous of Abe's connection to Nora! I was so jealous that Abe had taken Nora out on the river, for what would surely be her first time in a canoe that I could hardly breathe.

I stood on the river bank, trying my best to will them to come back, to include me. But there was no sound but a bob-o-link mocking me from a hollow dogwood on the opposite bank.

———

On Monday morning, the first thing I noticed was her sunburn. The tops of her arms and her collarbone were striped pink, and her freckles had multiplied and turned coppery. This small change in her appearance made me as crazy as if she'd shaved her head. As soon as we were alone, I hissed across the room at her: "Why the hell didn't you call me yesterday? You knew I'd be stressing about Abe!"

"Oh, he's not mad at you anymore, Pete," Nora assured me. "He was over it by the next morning. He got up and asked me if he could take me canoeing. He said it was a crime that I'd never been in a canoe before. We left early and we were gone all day."

I turned my back on her, trying to get control of my feelings. Behind me, she kept talking, "We rowed all the way from Elnora's Point to Abe's old neighborhood, Pete. I actually got to see the house my dad grew up in!"

I kept my back to her and sat behind my desk without speaking, until I heard her sigh with disappointment. By the time I looked up, she'd given up on me and was exiting the office; in the doorway she nearly collided with Bella, who was just coming in. "Hey, watch where you're going!" Bella scolded. Then she grinned at me, proud to have put Nora in her place.

"What is that girl's *problem*?" she asked, but this time I had no answer for Bella, knowing that today, the problem was me.

———

This was the day that Bella and I had scheduled to set Candy free in the woods, and Bella wanted to get right to it. "I'm worried about her," she confided as we headed out to the animal hospital. "What if she's forgotten how to be a fox?"

I had no such worry. The animal's foreleg was completely healed and she'd gained a little weight—her fur was bright orange and thick and her eyes were clear. She was ready. We settled her, still in her cage, into the back of my truck, and drove to the edge of the prairie, into a patch of wildflowers—prairie roses, brown-eyed susans, and day lilies. I opened the back end of the truck and invited Bella to unlatch the cage, which she did reluctantly. After a moment of sniffing at the opening of the cage, Candy scrambled out and took off, streaking across the prairie grass, a wild animal again, disappearing into the woods.

I had done this before with foundlings, and it was a moment that never failed to thrill me. I put a hand on Bella's shoulder and was surprised to feel it shaking under my hand. Bella was crying, and it seemed out-of-character. One of the things I most appreciated about her was her no-nonsense approach to the natural world. "The woods are Candy's real home," I reminded her.

"I don't know why I'm crying," she said. She wiped her eyes with the backs of her hands. "I hate myself for crying."

"It's okay, Bella-girl ... you can cry."

She shook her head, little fierce shakes. "Scientists don't cry," she said. Then she lifted her chin and stiffened her jaw. She kept her face locked like this on the ride back to the Visitor's Center, but I could tell from the way she was watching the scrub along the gravel road that she was looking for Candy.

———

Nora was at the river, sitting elbows-on-knees in the docked canoe. She stood up when she saw me, stepping out of the canoe and bracing herself for whatever attitude I was bringing her. I started my apology from some distance away. "I'm a jerk!" I called out to her. "I was jealous! Because I wish it had been me, taking you out for the first time in a canoe!"

Nora didn't answer, but her face registered surprise as I approached. "I don't know what's gotten into me, Nora! I don't know if this thing that's happening means anything to you. We had that one kiss and everything, and it's okay if it didn't mean anything, but I keep thinking about you ... all the time. I think about you ... "

As I came closer, Nora's expression became more intense and her eyes grew brighter. "I know I should have called you," she said. "I know I should have. But I wasn't myself. I needed to think. There were so many things. Things Abe told me." She stopped speaking and held up one hand, pointing to the river.

"What did he tell you?" I asked. I'd reached the place where she was standing and used her arms to tug her against me, until the length of her was pressed against the length of me. More softly, I asked, "What did he tell you?"

"My father's ashes are here," she said. "He'd put it in his will. His ashes are in the river." Then she lowered her head to my shoulder as if asking me to comfort her, something no girl had ever done with me before.

I melted. I held her against me with all my strength. Then she put her arms on my back and tipped her face to me, so I was sure she was not going to stop me from kissing her. And this was how we came to our second kiss—and it had the same electricity as the first, except this time we had the sun on our backs and river sounds all around us and I was not at all confused.

But as I lifted my hands to her shoulders, she flinched. "My sunburn—ouch! Ouch!"

"Sorry, sorry, sorry." My hands came back down slowly and found their way to the safe, hard triangle of her lower back as she lifted her arms to my shoulders. We clung in this new way and our mouths came easily together again. Until Nora pulled away and exclaimed, "I don't know when I'm leaving, Pete!"

"You're not leaving," I said, and covered her mouth with mine.

———

When I came back to the office, I heard back-and-forth accusations—Christina and Bella squabbling in the kitchen. Their voices rose, becoming angrier, and then the two of them were full-out arguing. "Would you just leave me alone!" Bella cried.

"Watch it, watch it, watch it!" Christina shrieked.

Then a crash, something shattering on the linoleum floor, and Christina cried, "Oh, for the love of God, Bella! Look at the mess you've made!"

Bella bolted from kitchen and ran past me into the yard. I found Christina on her hands and knees at the coffee machine, picking up shards of blue glass from a wide circle of spilt cocoa. "What happened?" I asked, kneeling to help her.

"Oh, she dropped a whole mug of cocoa. Might have

even burned her hand a little, I don't know. She wasn't being careful. She's *impossible* today! Now she'll be mad at me all afternoon."

"I think she was kind of upset about letting the fox go free. Should I see if she's okay?"

"Better you than me, my friend."

I found Bella in the animal hospital, sitting atop Candy's now-empty cage and wearing a miserable scowl, her dark eyebrows in a line. I approached her uncertainly. "Did you burn your hand?"

She was rubbing it. "Who cares if I did?"

"I do, Bella-girl!"

"Don't call me that!" Her face was suddenly splotched with anger. "I'm not a baby. And I'm so sick of this place, just really, really sick of it!" She was crying again, her face scrunched in misery, making no effort this time to hide her tears.

"Bella, Candy will be okay!"

"I'm not crying about a stupid fox!" Bella wailed. "*Everything* is wrong here. Everything is wrong because of *her*."

I knew she meant Nora, and I felt a wave of disloyalty, because only a few weeks ago I would have agreed with her. But before I could find my voice, Bella cried, "Nobody appreciates me!"

"That isn't true! I appreciate you like crazy!"

"Don't give me that bullshit," she said, surprising me with an adult curse. "I saw what you did. I saw the way you two were kissing. You *lied,* Pete. You said you didn't even *like* her."

Then I was at a complete loss for what to say. Bella had seen Nora and me basically making out in broad daylight. How could I even begin to explain? "I guess … I changed my mind … about her," I stammered.

Bella's face went several degrees wilder. "Oh YEAH? Well maybe I changed my mind about YOU!" She whirled away and I tried to touch her shoulder, but she jerked herself free. "I am not working here anymore! I QUIT!"

She left me with my mouth open and my arms hanging uselessly at my sides. After a few moments, I heard someone outside and Abe came wandering through the door, looking for birdseed. He greeted me with a little salute and a curt hello. I was relieved to see him. Sensible, silent Abe. The exact person I needed to hang with. The females around me were spinning out of control. I needed to be with my own kind.

———

We were filling bird feeders half an hour later, seeds, nuggets and suet—just the kind of task I needed after Bella's outburst, familiar and uncomplicated. No need for words. But Abe surprised me by being unusually talkative; he wanted to describe his day of canoeing with Nora—blow by blow, hour by hour, the way a little kid would tell you about a birthday party. At one point I interrupted impatiently, "Abe, *okay.* I've been in a canoe before."

"It wasn't just being in a canoe," Abe insisted quietly. "It was the memories. A landslide of memories, Pete. With every stroke of the oar. All these things I used to do with Paul. When we were kids—things I haven't let myself think about in a really long time."

"Good memories?"

"Yeah. The good ones. From before. Before things … got so … messed up."

"You mean before Nora's mom came."

He nodded ruefully. "But you know what I realized, Pete? It wasn't just Linda. I wasn't only fighting with Linda—that wouldn't have been so bad. The thing is—I was fighting with my brother. And the two of us—we had never fought about anything before that. He took care of me. He did everything for me. He was like … he was like …" Abe closed his eyes and couldn't finish.

"Until he met Linda," I prompted.

"Until Linda. And then all of a sudden they were always together and it was always the two of them, every day, and pretty soon she wanted things to change. She made it clear she didn't want me around. She told Paul it would never work if I was part of the deal. And I just knew she had given him some kind of ultimatum and I really hated her for it."

He turned to me then and put an urgent hand on my arm. "You can't ever tell Nora what I said just now, about her mom."

"Abe, she already knows you and her mom didn't get along. Even Gram and Gramps know that."

He shook his head. "Promise me you won't ever repeat what I said to you just now."

I promised. I had no problem with it. I liked that Abe was confiding in me on a new, adult level. I was proud to have a secret between us, even if it was about hating someone. What did it matter that I couldn't tell Nora something she already knew?

———

From the highest point of the ridge above Elnora's Point, I spotted her walking along the River Trail and called her name. Then I made my slippery way down the slope, through dogwood and spice bushes, to join her.

Her smile, at the sight of me, was beautiful to see. "I've been looking all over for you," she called. "Christina and Bella were arguing like crazy in the office. I had to get out of there. And here I thought they were the perfect mother and daughter!"

"Bella's mad at me," I reported glumly.

"Oh, she is *not*. She idolizes you."

"She knows about us, Nora. She saw us kissing at the river."

Nora's jaw dropped. "She saw us? What was she doing—*spying* on us?"

"She was probably just looking for me. She is my assistant."

"Oh please! That little *sneak*! She was spying on us!"

"Look, I don't want you to be mad at Bella," I said. "She's just ... she's just a kid. She can't help being jealous of you."

"Jealous of me?" Nora scoffed. "She's not jealous of me, Pete, she just doesn't like me. She's hated me since the day I arrived. She's just like my sister and her creepy little friends." She made a face, her fighter face, something I hadn't seen in a while. It changed the shape of her jaw and made her eyes flash.

"I really don't think … " I began.

"Forget it. I don't care—I'm used to having people hate me."

We walked in silence the rest of the way back to the Visitor's Center. I was still upset that I'd hurt Bella's feelings, and upset that Nora didn't sympathize. But it was more than that. I was mystified—I felt like someone on the outside, and wondered what it would be like to be so damn sure that the people around you hated you. What would that be like? What would it be like to have somebody in your own family hate you? And you hated them right back. It was so unknown to me—Gram and Gramps had always been so good to me, so easy, letting me decide what I needed and wanted, and when. I knew I was lucky. But on that walk I didn't feel lucky. I felt ignorant, and inexperienced and painfully different from the unlucky girl—braced for the next fight, ready for trouble—who walked so close beside me.

———

That same evening, Nora phoned and asked me to drive over and get her out of the cabin—something I was thrilled to do. When I pulled up, she hopped into the truck before I could get out and pulled a hand-drawn map out of her purse. "South of town," she commanded. "Take Red Bud Trail. And don't ask questions, just drive."

I followed these and other mysterious directions, and we traveled to a small subdivision on the outskirts of Buchanan. Nora consulted her map and directed me through the curving streets to a small bungalow. I recognized Christina's car in the narrow driveway. As soon as we pulled in, Bella opened the front door and came slouching out, her expression sullen. Christina appeared behind her, waved to us from the doorway, and mouthed *thank you*.

"Are we taking Bella somewhere?" I asked, surprised.

"Pizza," Nora announced. She got out and let Bella slide into the truck between us. It took us a few minutes to find the never-used middle seat belt, but once we had all buckled ourselves in, Bella gave me an icy stare. "I'm still quitting," she announced.

"I still don't want you to," I said.

She turned to Nora. "Did my mom ask you to do this?"

"Your mom had nothing to do with it," Nora insisted. "We just wanted to do something special with you before you leave town."

Bella's scowl deepened; she was unconvinced. "You guys just feel really guilty because I *saw* you. And you're afraid I'll tell everybody."

"We do not feel guilty and we don't care who you tell," Nora argued. "Tell whoever you want. Tell Abe, tell your mom, I don't care."

"Geez, I would never tell *her*!" Bella exclaimed, insulted. "She's in my face enough as it is!" She added, "Anyway, she'd probably think it was great. She thinks you're so interesting because you're Abe's niece. And she says I should be glad you came to Riverside because of how it changed Abe. She says he's more like a normal human being now."

This made me laugh, but when I looked at Nora, her expression was sad. "Maybe Nora will have the same effect on me," I suggested.

"I doubt it," Bella grumbled. "Where are you guys taking me for pizza?"

"We have a great place all picked out," I said, smiling at Nora over Bella's frizzy head, as though I had been in on the plan all along. We headed back into Buchanan. Nora asked if I could stop at an office supply store in one of the new strip malls. "I need a notebook," she told us. "Something with a cover."

"You mean like a diary?" Bella asked. "I write in a diary every day. Mine has a lock on it so my mom won't read it."

"My mom read my diary once," Nora reported softly. "Right before I came here, in fact."

"Was there bad stuff in it?"

"*Oh*, yeah." She grimaced.

"What do you need a diary now for?" Bella asked. "Oh, I know. To write about kissing Pete!"

Nora smiled but shook her head. "I just want to write down some of the things I'm learning."

"You mean so you won't forget everything when you go back to wherever it is you came from?"

"Indianapolis," Nora replied softly.

"So when *are* you going back? You've been here like *forever*."

"She doesn't know when she's going back," I insisted protectively.

"Will you be gone when I get back from visiting my dad?"

Nora hesitated a moment and then said, "Probably."

My heart sank. Nora stared out her window at the darkening sky.

Bella turned to me. "Will you be really sad when she goes?" she asked. Then she answered her own question. "He will. He'll be *really* sad. But he won't cry." She turned to Nora. "Scientists never cry."

"He'll miss me, though," Nora predicted. "And he'll miss you too, Bella."

"Will you really miss me, Pete?" Bella asked.

"Big time."

"You'll miss Nora more," she predicted. "You don't have to lie about it."

I looked at Nora over Bella's head, and it hit me all in a rush what it would mean to have no Nora at Riverside—something I had wanted so much in the beginning. I drove the rest of the way in silence, half-listening to Nora and Bella joking about Abe, joking about Christina, mock-insults and exclamations—what did it remind me of? Something I had seen on television or in the movies? Something about the way sisters act with each other? What did I know of sisters? What did I know about real families and their mysteries?

———

Nora got her notebook—lined pages with a cloth cover—and Bella forgave me and let me sit beside her in a booth at the pizza joint. We had a good pizza and a good time. After we'd dropped Bella back at her house, I said to Nora, "Is it just me, or was what happened just now kind of out-of-character for you?"

"You mean me being nice to Bella?" she asked. "Completely out-of-character. I can't even believe I thought of it. She's close to my sister's age, and I'm not exactly famous for being nice to *her*."

"Why do you hate your sister, Nora? Has it just always been that way?"

"It seems like it. We've always been so different. You'd have to meet her to understand. She actually looks like my mom in miniature—really pretty, with long curly brown hair and these huge brown eyes—and everyone treats her like a total princess. She has a great singing voice and she loves to perform in public, and all her grandparents and aunts and uncles think she's the most amazing kid ever born. And then there's me. The girl who nobody was ever quite sure where she came from, the girl nobody wanted around, the girl who was always in trouble."

"Was it really that bad?"

"Oh, sometimes. And when I came here, I honestly didn't care what happened to Carly. I was even hoping she'd finally have to suffer for a change, like I did."

"And is she suffering?"

"Oh God, she's just miserable. She called me crying a few days ago to tell me that things are pretty much over between her dad and my mom. And it turns out she's the only one who misses me. Carly! She actually misses me." Nora squeezed her eyes tightly shut and said, "Let's not talk about this anymore, okay?"

"Okay. But it's too early to go home. What do you want to do?"

"Something with you."

"Of course something with me."

"I know! Let's stay together until the moon comes out. Let's be in moonlight together. Moonlight on the river! You and me and a canoe in the moonlight, Pete. My first time canoeing after dark—how does that sound?"

I was thrilled. "God, it's a perfect night for it. There'll be a ton of moonlight in a few hours. But what about Abe?"

"What about Abe," she echoed. "Hmmm. I don't want Abe to wait up for me and worry again." She frowned, thinking. "Here's what we'll do. You take me home now and I'll wait for Abe to go to bed and sneak out after. I'll ride my bike to Riverside and meet you at the Visitor's Center. At midnight."

"Nora, are you sure you can get out without Abe hearing you?"

"Trust me, I'm a pro at sneaking out at night."

Which made me glance at her sideways, unsure that I liked hearing this.

"Sneaking out to do what exactly?"

"Don't ask."

———

It had been quite a while since I'd been in the woods after midnight. In many ways, I experienced it that night as though for the first time, all of the sounds and smells, the night sky alive and buzzing, the trees full of creatures, the surface of the pond pulsing. We saw bats flying between the trees and watched as a fox and a possum crossed our path. In the distance we could hear the splashing of animals leaving and returning to the river. I kept stopping on the trail to pull Nora close, to kiss her neck and nuzzle her hair and touch her warm skin. I felt like an animal myself, wildly alive, completely alert and happy.

The canoe was sitting in a circle of moonlight, as though expecting us. I stepped in first and Nora followed me; we sat facing each other and each took up a set of the old battered oars. "My father used these oars," she whispered. Off we went. The river took us, became like a living thing all around us, awakening with movement. Nora's face went in and out of shadows until, in the middle of the river, she sat in full moonlight, completely gorgeous. She threw her head back, holding fast to the oars, and laughed with joy.

I drank in the curve of her chin, her long neck, her strong

shoulders, and an urgent request came flying out of me, like our first kiss—unplanned and unstoppable: "Don't leave, Nora."

This brought her attention back to me. "Oh, Pete," she said.

"You know you don't want to!" I said. "You know you'll miss me as much as I'll miss you. You can live with Abe! You can go to high school here. He'll say yes. All you have to do is ask him."

Nora stopped rowing and lowered her head, getting upset. "You don't understand, Pete. There are things you don't know about me."

Her tone startled me, because I'd been feeling so close to her. "What don't I know about you?" I pleaded.

"Bad things happened, Pete. Before I came here. Stuff between me and my mom—it got really, really screwed up."

"I already know that! I know it was screwed up. She didn't even call you for weeks after you got here. And she never told you about Riverside. And she still hates Abe. Nora, these are all good reasons for you to just stay away from her!"

Her eyes flashed. "That's easy for you to say! You don't have a mother!"

This hurt me. "Gram is my mother," I said.

"I'm not talking about your gram," she said. "I'm talking about my mom. Somebody who a few months ago wanted to kill me. And now she totally needs me. And I can't just cut her off and pretend she doesn't exist. She's out there somewhere. She's coming after me. And she's going to really need me, now that it seems she's alone again. She hates to be alone."

"But you said you don't want to be like her. And you said being here has changed you!"

I said this urgently, because I realized in a flash that we had changed together. Something had taken hold of the two of us, something I didn't completely understand, but I could not bear the thought of it ending. And I was afraid that if Nora did leave Riverside, it *would* end. I might not see her again for a long time—maybe never. All that had happened this summer would fade, and she would become one of the things in my past I refused to look back on. "Don't leave me, Nora," I pleaded.

But she stayed silent, her head lowered so that I could not see her face. And just at that very moment, a fluttering shadow fell across the canoe. I looked up and saw in the moonlight a gigantic moth—a slow-moving, iridescent *Luna*—circling Nora's head. "Look up," I whispered.

She did. Then she gasped and followed the creature with her eyes, her mouth a silent "O." We watched in silence for what seemed like forever. *Actius Luna* flapped and fluttered away, searching for a mate.

"It's a sign," I whispered. I remembered something I'd read in one of Gram's lepidoptery books and I spoke it aloud: "The Pottawatomi believed that moths were sent from the moon with messages from the dead!"

Nora began to row again.

"Was that a little too morbid for you?"

"Nothing's too morbid for me anymore. But what if the message is a warning? From the river. From my father."

This gave me a chill. "What would he be warning us about?" I wondered.

"About my mom coming. Coming to get revenge, and it will be my fault because of everything I stirred up, coming here."

Again, I thought of what Gram had said—*she brought something only she could bring.* "Why does your mom still need revenge?" I asked.

"There's something Abe's not telling us," Nora continued. "There must be some other reason why he's afraid of my mom. Something that's stuck deep inside of him."

"Nora, they just never liked each other," I insisted gently.

Nora was shaking her head. "There's more, there's more."

"I really think he's told us everything."

"People can't always tell everything," she argued. "Sometimes they have to leave things out so that they can … recover. Start over. So that people will still be able to love them."

There was something so pleading in her tone and her expression that I was afraid to press her about what she meant. I rowed us back to Elnora's Point in silence, and I helped her out of the canoe without a word. On the path, we held hands tightly but stayed separate in our silences.

When I'd pulled the truck as far into Abe's driveway as I dared, I reached across the front seat, grabbed her shoulders, and kissed her—and she kissed me back, but it was a different kiss than we'd shared before. It was as though we were kissing each other across a great space that had opened up between us—the things we weren't sure of, the things she wouldn't tell me, whatever was coming, and the possibility that she would leave.

Moth Journal

Paul McMichael

Buchanan, Michigan

November 1988

Push an insect pin through the center of the thorax of a freshly killed moth. (If the insect has dried, use a relaxing jar to soften it.) One fourth of an inch of the pin should show above the thorax. Make sure the insect does not tip from side to side or front to back on the pin. Push the pin straight down into the board until the outstretched wings are just level with the surface of the board.

Now insert a pin lightly in each front wing near the front margin and behind a wing vein. Move the front wings forward gently until the hind margins of the front wings are in a straight line. Now move the hind wing forward until the gap between front and hind wing is closed.

If using a specimen from the relaxing jar: Remove the insect carefully with forceps (never touch the wing surface with your fingers). Then, holding moth by the thorax, carefully force an insect pin through the middle of the body, between the wings. Pin the specimen onto the mounting board, being careful to keep the wing hinge above the surface of the mounting board. Wings can then be secured with pins. Make sure antennae and abdomen are in proper position before pinning. Check overall position of the specimen. Make adjustments before placing wider strips of paper over the wings to prevent curling during the drying period.

Yesterday I ordered ten hardwood 5" X 6" display cases; I decided to display the moths individually rather than put them all together in one big frame. Once they are labeled and under glass they will be more impressive and diverse as individual specimens, although I may want to put some of the smaller ones together in the same case. Must ask Mrs. Shelton what she thinks about this. The state science competition application deadline is next week. I have caught and pinned twenty-seven moths, but some are duplicates; I must choose the best specimen of each moth; Mrs. Shelton can help me do this. My task now is to stay focused and dedicated and not let any of the things that are going wrong in my life distract me, because I am going to go to that science fair and I am going to win.

August 2006

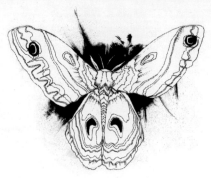

12. Pupae

The last month of the summer arrived on a wave of dry heat with record highs. The river current crawled under a cloud of warm air that wouldn't lift and seemed to thicken at dusk, when the frogs and crickets went into a frenzy of noise. In the mornings, the office fans couldn't cut through the heat, and this, combined with the fact that Christina and Bella weren't bustling in and keeping us motivated, put the three of us into a kind of trance. We came in and basically just hung out together, walking in and out of buildings without purpose and accomplishing almost nothing.

But we didn't mind—nobody was complaining. We'd slowed down in the heat like the animals, drinking water and trying our best to stay comfortable. I don't think any of us wanted to face the fact that the time we three were sharing in that heat wave wouldn't last.

In the midst of this, Abe decided that he and Nora should try camping; he called it "perfect weather for sleeping on the river"—late sunset, still nights, and fewer bugs than we'd had earlier in the summer because it was bone dry. I found Nora in the basement of the Visitor's Center, where we stored an assortment of tents and sleeping bags and other old camping gear, everything wrapped in heavy trash bags. She was making a stack of things they would need, and she told me that she'd never slept outside before.

"Your mom *never* took you camping?" I asked in disbelief. "What about all those trips up north?"

"We stayed in motor lodges, Pete. Cheap motels. My mom is the most not-outdoorsy person you could ever meet."

"I don't get it, Nora. If this place was so important to your dad—"

"I know," she interrupted. "I'm going to ask her how in the world they ever got together, don't worry."

She said it like this would be happening soon. The dismay I felt must have shown on my face, because she moved across the basement, threw her arms around me, and planted her first kiss of the day. It had become a kind of game with us—figuring out when and where we could kiss and not be seen by Abe, who must have known by then how we felt about each other.

Later that same day, I asked Abe if I could tag along on

his camping trip with Nora. We were in the kitchen of the Visitor's Center. He looked up from the newspaper he was reading and frowned. "Why do you want to come?"

"Abe, it's me, your *old* camping buddy, remember?"

"I suppose you could pitch a tent a few yards away," he grumbled.

"A few yards? Should I bring a tape measure?" I asked. He either didn't get it or didn't respond.

Nora was measuring coffee into the coffee maker; she overheard, glanced my way, and rolled her eyes. After Abe had left the kitchen, she said, "He's so ... I don't know ... *protective* of me. It's *so* not what I'm used to."

"No? What are you used to?"

She looked away.

"Why can't you tell me what you're used to?"

"Pete, don't start."

"So you're not used to men being protective of you—big deal. Is that supposed to shock me?"

"Really, Pete," she insisted quietly. "Change the subject."

"Are you afraid I can't handle it? Like I'm too ... innocent?"

"You *are* innocent, okay? It's one of the reasons I trust you."

I groaned, aggravated, and she pulled me close to cheer me up and studied my face. "It's one of the reasons I love you. That and your eyes. They have this shine in them, a sparkle, but they're kind of sad, too. And they show all these hidden colors when you stand in the light."

I shut my eyes, frustrated that she was blatantly flattering me to change the subject, but also weakening.

"Hey, you," she said. "Come back. What are you thinking?"

"Eyespots," I said. "I'm thinking eyespots."

"You mean moths?" she asked hopefully. "Is it finally okay for us to talk about moths?"

"Change the subject," I replied, but softened my request by kissing her nose.

———

When I told Gram at dinner that I was going to be camping on the river for a few days with Abe and Nora, she took the news calmly. "Oh, so you're *freely* choosing to spend time with Nora now?"

"Abe will be there too," I pointed out.

"Well, of *course.*"

Gramps caught my eye. "Your grandmother and I are wondering if we can assume that you are not having such a hard time being around a certain person these days."

"That's not all I'm wondering," Gram said quietly.

I kept my eyes on my plate. "Things are getting better," I confessed vaguely. "But it's still kind of complicated."

"Perhaps it's complicated," Gramps said. "Or perhaps it's very simple."

At this Gram and I exchanged a private glance of silent agreement: *it's definitely not simple.*

———

And so we spent the next few days in the same, slow pattern with one difference—we ended each day at our little campsite on the river. We grilled fish and chicken over a fire pit and listened to Abe share St. Joseph River history, stuff I'd heard many times before but didn't mind hearing again, since I knew it was all new to Nora. How the river spanned over two hundred miles; how it had been an important canoe route for the Pottawatomis and the early fur traders, a crucial canoe route between the watersheds of the Mississippi and Lake Michigan. How dramatically it zigs and zags, flowing both north and south in our little corner of Michigan, a geographic anomaly. I knew it all and I sat on a log and listened anyway, watching Nora's profile in the fading light, appreciating her occasional husky laugh and her heartfelt questions. Sometimes she teased Abe about how much more he knew about his property and the river than about real people; she could make him laugh in a way I'd never heard him laugh before.

When it was pitch dark and the moon was high, we would disappear into the trio of tents we'd pitched, mine a slight distance apart from Nora's and Abe's as Abe had requested. In the morning I would wake up first and start coffee, listening for the first sounds of Nora stirring in the cocoon of her tent, watching her emerge in pajamas and unlaced boots, her face slightly puffy, her hair crazy. This would be our moment. If we stood behind Abe's tent, and if Abe was still asleep, then it was safe to kiss her and press her body against mine while she was still warm and fragrant from her sleeping bag. It was like stepping out of time, those few days in that heat, on that river. It was bliss.

———

On the third day, Abe and I left Nora behind to clean up the site; we headed to the office and cold showers in the upstairs bathroom at the Center. It was just after nine a.m. and already way too hot. Abe was working at his desk in the sweltering heat when I came down from my shower, still shirtless, already working up a new sweat.

"Let's work on the porch today," I suggested.

He brought his invoices and I brought my sketchpad and that's where we were sitting when we saw, from a distance, Nora walking back toward the Visitor's Center with a bag of trash over one shoulder. "The girl's a born camper," Abe said appreciatively. "Look at her. She loves the river, just like Paul did."

"Abe, I've been wondering about something," I said. "I've been wondering how your brother and Nora's mom ever got together in the first place. It doesn't sound like they had very much in common."

"They sure didn't."

"How did they even meet?"

"I'm not sure exactly. I guess … at that point in his life he was just … ready to meet someone. I hear that what you do or don't have in common doesn't matter so much at the beginning."

"Abe, he *chose* her. And Christina says he was really handsome and that lots of girls were interested in him. So why did he choose a girl who was so different from him?"

"Christina told you that?"

"She remembers him from high school. You should ask her about it sometime."

He looked completely befuddled to hear this. "She remembers Paul?"

"So, why did he get married so young? To somebody like Linda?"

Abe focused on my question again. "It was a strange time for him, I think—that year after he graduated. He didn't have to work. Our mom had left him enough money and he was mostly taking care of me. We were living in the house I grew up in, and I was still in school. I think he just really needed ... someone. I think there was an emptiness inside of him. And then there was Linda—right in front of him, ready to fill the emptiness. She was ... pretty. Kind of wild, wilder than him, anyway. And there was Riverside. She knew it was Paul's, and she knew it was worth a lot of money. I always believed ... it was a factor."

Nora was getting closer. She waved to us. "Don't you tell Nora what I just said about her mother and the money," Abe requested softly.

Moth Journal

Paul McMichael

Buchanan, Michigan

December 1988

Female moths are often larger than male moths, with more rounded forewings and bigger abdomens if they are carrying eggs. Since they are not always seen together, there are other ways to tell them apart. The most obvious difference is the antennae; male silk moths typically have broad comb antennae, while the female has a narrower, more threadlike one. Male moths have a wider diversity of antennae than females, but it is safe to say that the female antennae are longer, while the males are broader and more feathery. Which is one of the reasons I prefer male specimens for mounting and display to females—the combs give them a more dramatic and mysterious look under glass and reveal (I think) one of the things I love most about moths—that they have this kind of radar apparatus attached to their flying bodies, part science, part magic. It allows them to function beautifully in darkness without ears, without mouths, and without sight or memory as we know it.

They are designed for brief, crazy, urgent, untraceable life, and they are beautiful seen and beautiful unseen, and whether or not we notice them, they fly and thrive and breed and return. Could they be more amazing, more strange, more puzzling?

13. Flight

It was rare for a car to roll up to the Visitor's Center unexpectedly. At the first crunch of gravel, I moved to the office window and watched a blue sedan pull into the parking lot—a Honda with a blaring radio, classic rock, something by the Rolling Stones. Behind the wheel sat a woman leaning her head slightly out the window, a woman I didn't know. She had hoop earrings and big sunglasses, red lips, and black hair twisted up high at the back of her head.

I came out onto the front porch and she turned off her engine, opened her door, got out of the car, and took off her sunglasses. Very dark eyes and eyebrows.

"Is there an Abe McMichael inside?" she called.

It was as though Nora's voice was coming out of this stranger's mouth! It startled me so thoroughly that I lowered my head a moment, collecting my wits. "Ahh ... he's not here," I managed to say.

"Anybody else around?" she asked and I told her no, which was true.

"Nora's not there with you?" she pressed, slightly teasing.

I shook my head.

"Know who I am?"

I put my hands in my pockets nervously and nodded. She was amused by my awkwardness; her smile had stayed in place throughout the exchange, curving down on one side— Nora's smile.

"Wow, she never mentioned having such a cute boy around," Linda said. "Any idea where I can find her this morning?"

"She's probably still at Abe's," I said. "He lives just up the road."

"Is he there too?"

"No, he's in Buchanan running errands."

"Oh good. Tell me again where he lives."

"Turn right as you leave Riverside and go down a couple of miles. There's a log cabin on the left. You can't miss it."

"You're very sweet. One more thing. Could you recommend a good place to get breakfast on our way out of town? I drove most of the night and I'm starving."

Our way out of town? I thought, my heart sinking. I struggled to stay composed and said, "There's probably food at the cabin."

"I'm in kind of a rush. I didn't catch your name ... ?"

"I'm Pete Shelton," I said. "Abe's assistant."

"Shelton?" she repeated. "Pete ... *Peter* Shelton? Wait a minute, you're not that boy who ... that girl, the girl who ran off and left ...?"

She paused, searching her memory. "I remember you! From when the Sheltons first adopted you. Paul told me about it. What was her ... what was your mother's name?"

"Rose," I said. It was such an unfamiliar word that my voice cracked as I said it. I looked over my shoulder, at the phone, wanting to call Nora.

"Wow, take a look at you now," she continued. "All grown up. Strange that Nora never mentioned you. Or is it?"

The teasing smile again.

"I have to get back to work," I said uneasily.

"So are Ida and Conrad still alive?" she asked bluntly.

"Oh yeah. They're fine. I live with them, right down the road."

Her expression turned sympathetic. "Poor you. Well, give them my very best, won't you? Tell them Linda from Indianapolis says hello. Gotta run!"

She dropped back behind the wheel of her car and re-started the engine. I was backing away; I even stumbled slightly on my way to the phone, dialing the cabin as the sound of her engine faded down the road.

———

Ten minutes later, I saw the same woman again, this time in Abe's kitchen—a mother and daughter reunion, the two of them looking, as Nora had predicted, not the slightest bit related. Everything about them was a contrast—their sizes, their hair, their eyes, their profiles—but they were staring each other down with the same set jaws, the same stubbornness. Nora was sitting at the table, still in her pajamas, eyes puffy, hair a wild mop. A bowl of gone-soggy cereal waited on the table in front of her.

She'd begged me on the phone to come right over, to help her to deal with her mother. But now she sent me an uncertain look, as though beginning to doubt that having me there was a good idea.

"What is *he* doing here?" Linda demanded. "Oh, I get it. You invited him over. Cute guy, Nora. Your latest?"

Nora shot me a look I couldn't decipher. "He's my friend," she said.

"He's a *Shelton*. Has anyone here mentioned what the Sheltons did to me?"

"I could wait outside," I suggested unhappily, but Nora sent me another piercing look, this one loud and clear: *don't leave me!*

"Although to be fair, Pete here is not related by blood to the Shelton family," Linda went on. "So we can't very well blame him for how the Sheltons screwed us over, can we?"

She turned to me, and her smile was dangerous. Yet I sensed that she was also afraid. I had an impulse to pull up a chair beside Nora and put a protective arm around her, but the energy in the room was so thick that it seemed like any sudden movement might cause an explosion. So I stayed in the doorway, my arms crossed, and kept a close watch on Nora's face.

"I don't care what the Sheltons did to you, Mom," Nora cried. "I don't care that you didn't get half of Riverside. I just want to know why you never told me about it."

"There was nothing to tell!" Linda exclaimed. "Everything was gone! There was nothing to tell you about. And I swore I would never come back here, but God help me, here I am, back in the town that time forgot. Which my daughter has decided is her new playground. Because—big surprise—she's found herself another boyfriend."

"Mom, quit talking about him like he's not even here!"

"Oh, I know he's here. And I'm sure you've been having way too much fun with him."

This I couldn't let go by. "I'm not the reason she stayed here, Mrs. McMichael," I said.

She turned to me. "McMichael?" she scoffed. She turned to her daughter. "Did you tell everyone here your name is McMichael? Oh, very nice touch, Nora."

Nora covered her face.

"Our last name is Cobb," Linda said. "And it's very possible that you don't know Nora Cobb as well as you think you do. But one thing hasn't changed. She sure likes to have a man around, don't you, Nora? But isn't this one a little young for you?"

Nora moved her hands from her eyes to her ears, blocking this question. Linda stepped closer to Nora, leaning over the table and putting her face in line with her daughter's. She grabbed Nora's chin, a rough gesture that Nora endured. "Nora prefers older men, don't you, Nora?"

"You left me alone with him," Nora said from between her teeth. "How could you do that—you knew what he was like."

I was fighting an impulse to cover my ears. But too late. I heard, and I knew. Perhaps I had already known. Not a random older man with a car. Not just someone married. Her own stepfather. This was the crime she couldn't tell me about. The reason she had run away.

People can't always tell everything.

Sometimes they have to leave things out ... so that people will still be able to love them.

You don't want to know.

Nora was crying.

"I told you," her mother said, letting go of her face. "I told you I've forgiven you for all the incredibly stupid things you did to hurt me. I forgave you a long time ago. But get this through your head. I am not letting you stay in this town another minute. I don't care how much you suddenly love it here. Get your things. And I am not asking you, I'm telling you. Get ... your ... THINGS."

Nora lowered her head. "I need to talk to Pete."

"Oh, I don't think so. You need to start packing."

"We won't go anywhere," I promised quietly. "We just need to talk. Just let us say goodbye. I'll help her pack. Give us an hour."

Linda looked first at Nora, then at me—a mistrustful

look, but I saw that she was wavering. She grabbed her purse from Abe's kitchen counter and slung it over one shoulder. As she passed me in the doorway, she said, "One hour. And if you two try to pull anything on me, you'll both be sorry. Do you understand? Do you understand me, Nora?"

When we were sure that she was gone, Nora pushed her cereal bowl back from the table's edge and buried her head in her arms. I came to the back of her chair, bent over her, and wound my arms around her shoulders. She leaned sideways, wrapped her own arms over mine, and clung to me. "Now you know," she said.

"Yep," I said. "I know it all."

"I told you it would be bad."

"That was … pretty bad."

"She's on the rampage, Pete. We have to keep her away from Abe."

Abe. I had forgotten about Abe. Now I felt a wave of relief that he was not around. None of the anger set loose in his cabin had been aimed at him. I felt a surge of my old protectiveness toward him. And it came to me that the only way to protect Abe from damage in this situation was for Nora to leave with her mother. Disappear—both of them.

I pulled Nora to her feet and put my arms around her. It was a goodbye embrace; we both knew it.

"I have to get ready," she said.

"Let me help you," I agreed. I led her by the hand into her little room. She sat on her bed and pulled off her T-shirt, seemingly unaware of her own nakedness. I found a clean shirt and handed it to her, and she pulled it over her head. I pulled her old duffel out from under the bed and began filling it with her clothes, both clean and dirty. Nora stood up shakily and starting putting toiletries into her backpack.

After a few moments, we heard a car approaching. It was Abe. He called Nora's name from the driveway.

"Is that Pete in there?" he called. He sounded angry. *Angry at me*, I realized. Because he'd seen my truck and knew I was alone in the cabin with Nora.

"Get him out of here," Nora whispered.

"I will," I promised. "Leave as soon as your mom comes back. I'll explain it to him later."

"Goodbye, Pete," she said. The word sounded so feeble. I hugged her once more, briefly, hopelessly, before hurrying out of her room to meet my accuser.

———

I made a lame, convoluted excuse about why I was at the cabin and asked Abe to take me back to Riverside right away. I was braced for whatever he would say to me about being alone with Nora, but for the first few moments he was silent. And I was also silent, still in shock, struggling to handle what had just happened.

"We have to talk about this," Abe said finally.

"Right," I agreed.

"We have to talk about you and Nora. We have to have rules."

"Right, okay."

"Just because the two of you have become … closer lately, that doesn't mean that … "

He stopped then, his attention distracted by an oncoming blue Honda. I held my breath, praying that Abe wouldn't recognize the woman behind the wheel. Beside me, I heard him inhale sharply. He put his foot to the brakes and skidded us to a dusty stop. I watched his face, saw a transformation take place on his broad features—realization, disbelief, fear. Behind us, Thor began to bark.

"Why are we stopping?" I asked, pretending not to know.

Abe began shifting gears, reversing and accelerating to turn the jeep around.

"What are you doing?" I asked, although I knew what he was doing. When he had turned the car completely around, he gunned the engine.

"Where are we going?" Although, of course, I knew that too.

——

"Oh, just perfect!" Linda exclaimed from the porch as Abe and I pulled up to the cabin. "Now we've got both of them!"

She was holding the screen door ajar while Nora lugged her duffel through the doorway. At the sight of us, Nora dropped the duffel and straightened; the look she sent me was full of dismay. Abe got out from behind the wheel, took in the situation, and stood in the drive, unsure of what to do. Thor, caught inside the jeep, was barking like an attack dog at the stranger on the front porch.

"Thor, be quiet!" Abe commanded, but his voice was full of fear. He did not greet Linda at all; instead, he looked past her to Nora. "Nora?" he asked. "Are you leaving?"

"Damn right, she's leaving," Linda answered sharply. "She's had enough of this awful place, just ask her."

After a silent pause, Abe said forlornly, "Have you had enough of this awful place, Nora?"

At the sadness in his voice, Nora left her duffel in the doorway and rushed headlong down the porch steps to where Abe was. As he folded Nora into an embrace, I saw something come unhinged in Nora's mother. She came roaring down the steps too, her face contorted with rage, her voice suddenly completely hysterical. "Get away from her!" she shrieked. "Get away from her or I'll call the police!"

"Mom!" Nora cried. "Stop screaming!"

"Get away from her or I'll tell her what you did!"

Nora had her arms around Abe's waist, but I saw his back stiffen.

"Get your hands off her!" Linda screamed. Nora finally turned from Abe's embrace, faced her mother, and yelled back: "I don't care what he did! It wasn't as bad as what you did to me! Never bringing me here! Never telling me about my dad!"

Linda froze in her tracks, a few yards away from them. "You think what I did was so bad? You think I'm the bad guy here?" She looked past Nora, into Abe's eyes, which I could see were full of dread. "She doesn't know, does she? She doesn't know how her father died. That was one story you didn't get around to telling her, wasn't it?"

"What don't I know?" Nora howled. "Somebody tell me!"

"Ask your uncle!"

Abe sagged where he stood and put one hand on the hood of his jeep for support. At this Linda took another step closer and pushed Nora aside, so that she and Abe were face-to-face at last. "Tell her why he went out in that storm," Linda said. "Tell her what you said to him!"

Abe looked at Nora pleadingly. Everyone was waiting. Even Thor had stopped barking.

"You can tell me," Nora said softly.

"We were fighting," Abe said. "We were always fighting then. This one was bad. I was so mad at him. I told him that he wasn't my brother anymore. I told him I didn't want to see him ever again! And then I left. I left our house and I walked out into the storm. And he came looking for me. He was coming to find me and bring me back."

"Of course he was," Nora said, starting to cry. "Of course he was coming to find you."

"You destroyed him!" Linda cried. "You said those terrible things and it made him crazy. That's why he was driving so fast. I begged him not to go. I begged him to just wait." She pointed to Abe, her voice rising to a shriek. "He might as well have killed him himself!"

"NO!" Nora screamed. She covered her ears and ran back inside.

After a frozen moment, all of us staring at where Nora had just been, I rushed into the cabin to find her, barreling through the rooms and calling her name. There was no sign of her in her newly empty bedroom, nothing left but the bedding and the moths on the walls. Back in the kitchen, I noticed that the back door of the cabin was slightly ajar. From the window above the kitchen sink, I saw a flash of bright blue—Nora's backpack—moving in a line down Rangle Road. Someone speeding away on a bicycle.

Linda and Abe were still outside, waiting for whatever I would say. I stayed in the cabin, giving Nora a few minutes of escape time before coming back out onto the porch to tell them I couldn't find her. "The bike is gone. She's probably heading over to Riverside."

"Go and get her," Linda said, but in her tone was more plea than command.

I glanced at Abe. He nodded. I hesitated, unsure whether I should leave him alone with Linda.

"I'm all right," Abe said, reading my mind. "Go and find her."

Linda added, "Bring her to me. I need her." Then she put a hand over her mouth to cover a long sob and walked back to her sedan. She got behind the wheel and lowered her head into her arms.

I looked at Abe again. He said quietly, "She'll be all right too. The main thing now is Nora."

"Do you want to come with me?"

He shook his head. He was leaning against the shiny hood

of his jeep. "I can't face her," he said. "Just … you go." It was the voice of a defeated man.

———

The bike was leaning against the outside of the Visitor's Center, but there was no sign of Nora inside. I searched the house and then the outbuildings, then hiked down to the river, all to no avail. I spent the rest of the afternoon, walking the trails at Riverside—sometimes calling Nora's name so that she would know I was around, sometimes keeping silent, watching for a sign of her … any sign … a shadow through the trees, a branch moving, a glimpse of blue backpack, or the bright flash of her hair.

At dusk I settled tiredly onto the bench at Elnora's Point, realizing that Nora probably knew I was searching for her. I considered the possibility that she did not want to be found. That she might prefer to stay hidden for a while. Consider her next move. The three of us would just have to wait.

Moth Journal

Paul McMichael

Buchanan, Michigan

January 1989

All that is left to do is frame the last few specimens, finish the display panels, gather up notes for my presentation and write my final paper. I am overwhelmed, but confident. I also feel an anxiousness, a coming emptiness. I can't help wondering what will take the place of this amazing project? What will fill my days when I am truly finished?

I have learned that moths are nature's masters of disguise. Some take on the appearance of leaves, shed skin, assorted garbage—all to hide from their enemies; several of the family of Noctuidae have wing colors and patterns that actually look like bird droppings. This is how they hide and survive!

Some moths look so much like other insects. The hornet moth looks like a yellowhead, the entire family Sesiidae resemble assorted wasps, and the plume moth is easily mistaken for a crane fly. In fact, the appearance of many moths suggest the features of animals and birds, and the moths are named accordingly—the Monkey Moth, the Peacock Moth, the Hummingbird Clearwing, the mighty Hawkmoths (including the Elephant Hawkmoth of Asia, its body tapering to a kind of trunk—amazing!). The huge Owl Moths of India and Japan have wings that are so much like the face of an owl that even the human eye is tricked.

Was there ever a creature put on God's earth more suited to looking like something besides what it actually is? Moths are tricksters! Another reason to be amazed by them. I finish my displays in a constant state of awe.

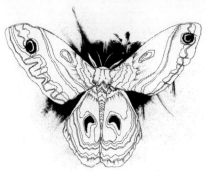

14. Trickster

"You called out for Abe in your sleep several times during the night," Gram said. "You haven't done that since you were a little boy."

We were eating breakfast on the porch because of the heat—Gram and I side by side in the swing, Gramps sitting upright on the top step. We held our plates in our laps as I described most of what had happened yesterday, leaving out what I'd learned about Nora and her stepfather. "You were right about us needing to be ready," I told Gram. "None of us were ready, not really."

"So much fresh pain after all these years," Gram sighed. "No wonder the girl had to run from it."

"You know, we always had a feeling that she blamed Abe for the accident," Gramps said, "although we didn't fully understand why. Abe never spoke to us about that night—we didn't ask him to. We wanted to help him put it behind him. Now the truth comes out."

"She was wrong to accuse him in front of Nora," Gram said. "But if he's been carrying that burden of guilt all these years, then perhaps it's better for both of them that it's all out in the open now."

"She seemed crazy," I said.

"She lost so much in this town, son," Gramps insisted gently. "More than enough to make a person crazy."

He looked over his shoulder at Gram and they exchanged a look I didn't recognize—guilt? Regret?

But then Gram spoke and her voice was fierce. "I couldn't let her have Riverside, Peter. It wouldn't have been right. I had to do what I did for Elnora."

"It went deeper than that, Ida," Gramps chided. "Tell the boy why you felt so strongly about it."

Gram stopped the swing and put down her plate. She spoke without looking at either of us. "We'd sold the property to Elnora, knowing it would fall to Paul after she died. It was time for us to move on, but there was another reason we sold it when we did. Elnora was angry at me; she thought I had taken her son away from her, that fall. It was because of the moths. I thought he needed them, and I encouraged him. Guided him. Kept him with me in the lab after school. Once I realized how much I'd hurt her, I was desperate to make it right. I needed to offer Riverside to her so that she could leave Paul something even more important than what

I'd given him. And it made things right again, between us, before she died. I was so grateful for that."

She rummaged in the pocket of her gardening smock for a Kleenex, found one, and dabbed her eyes. "Ah, but there was a cruelty in it," she continued. "A terrible cruelty. Taking a stand like that against a young woman who was already in so much pain."

Gramps added softly, "It was such a difficult time, Peter. Like a tunnel we thought we would never find our way out of. And I suppose some of us never did."

Then we were all silent for a moment, lost in our own thoughts. Beside me, Gram wiped her eyes one last time, and began to move the swing again, slightly. "Do you think Nora is staying close to the river, Peter?" she asked.

"I do," I said. "There are signs…"

"Signs," she repeated. "Did you know that sleeping near the river after a battle is an ancient rite?"

I'd heard this from Gram before, and I nodded and put my hand over the nearest of hers.

"I used to recommend it all the time to my students, but only a few ever listened. Nora is a true McMichael. Her father and her grandmother would be so proud of her."

I didn't get up. I didn't bolt for my room to avoid an emotional moment. I stayed on the swing beside my Gram. Gramps and I looked at each other, a long moment. Man-to-man. I didn't want any one of us to move just yet.

———

At ten a.m. the temperature was up to ninety degrees and the office was sweltering. I heard a car coming, above the drone of the fan, and I braced myself. A few moments later, Linda appeared at the screen door wearing cutoffs and a T-shirt, her hair straight and loose; it hung clear to the middle of her back. Today she looked like a teenager, except for her face—puffy and wrinkled under a layer of makeup.

I was wary. I waited for her to come inside, but for a long moment she just stood, silently staring at the office through the screen.

"Door's open," I called.

She took a halting step, looking around. "Man, you would not believe how weird it feels to step into this old house again."

"You remember it?"

She nodded. "Oh my God, yes. Although the place was empty when I met Paul. The Sheltons had already moved out, but they were still taking care of it. Paul lived in a house in town with his brother."

She came farther into the room, cringing visibly as though she expected something to fall on her head from above. "Yeah, he brought me over here a few times. Wanted me to see where his big old nature center would be one day. I acted interested. I was a good sport about it." She crossed her arms tightly across her chest and made her way slowly to the space behind my desk—to my bulletin board, where she peered at my drawings a little suspiciously, the same way Nora had on the day she'd first come over to the Center. I watched her from the corner of my eye, realizing that despite how rough she looked today, she'd probably been truly gorgeous when Paul had first met her.

She turned and caught me staring. She smiled. "So, have you talked to Nora yet?" she asked brightly.

"Haven't seen her," I replied, and it was true.

She came around to the front of my little desk and leaned over it slightly. Involuntarily, I found myself leaning backwards, away from her. "You know, Pete, I'm very sorry about what happened yesterday," she said. "I didn't come back to Buchanan to make a scene like that. Honestly, I don't know what got into me." She hesitated, and added, "Well, actually I do know. But I didn't mean to go off like that in front of everybody. I hope you can believe me."

I changed the subject. "Where did you end up staying last night?"

"Turns out an old friend of mine still lives here in town. A distant cousin—Rita. The same cousin I was spending the summer with when I met Nora's father. Anyway, talk about a time warp. Rita is still living in the same house, has three kids, and is twice divorced. She said I could stay with her until we work this thing out, Nora and me."

She was staring at my fern drawings—woodferns, walking ferns, polypody. "You drew these?" she asked, looking over my shoulder.

I nodded.

"You take after your mom, huh?"

I must have looked surprised. "The artist thing," she explained. "Your mom was one too."

"How do you know that?"

She shrugged. "I don't know. I never met her. Paul must have told me. I guess they were pals for a little while, before she took off. She liked the bugs and the flowers and that whole knowing-the-names-of-birds thing."

Ornithology. Had anyone ever told me this? In a faraway place in my mind, it seemed like something I used to know. She was a scientist. She was more of an artist than a scientist. She ran off to Idaho and never came back.

"She never came back here?" Linda asked, as if reading my thoughts. "After she joined that religious cult or whatever it was?"

I hesitated for a long moment, and then I asked calmly, "It was a religious cult?"

"I'm pretty sure. Somewhere out of state. Iowa? Idaho? Didn't the Sheltons ever tell you?"

"It's been a long time since it's come up, actually. I just ... I don't generally talk about her."

"Yeah, it was one of those cults that were big in the eighties. Where you cut off all past ties. Crazy stuff. Although believe me, I knew plenty of people who did crazy stuff back then. Like me, for instance. Moving to the middle of nowhere and hooking up with a nature guy. A man I had nothing in common with."

"Why did you marry him?"

"Silly boy. I was crazy in love."

"But you just said you didn't have anything in common with him."

"So I *pretended*." She was pacing now. "Pretended to love, love, love the great outdoors. It was an Oscar-winning performance. That's what you do when you fall in love with somebody who's really, really different from you, Pete. You pretend."

I didn't like where the conversation was going. "Nora's not pretending," I insisted quietly.

"Well—she's one fast learner, you have to admit that much!" Linda came back to my desk and leaned over it, her face too friendly. "So where did our favorite girl sleep last night?"

"I don't know. I told you, I haven't seen her."

"Where do you *think* she slept?"

"Somewhere on the other side of the river. The canoe's gone. And there's a tent and a sleeping bag missing from the basement."

"My daughter sleeping in a tent? Oh, honey, I don't think so."

I shrugged, unwilling to argue.

"You're a nice kid, Pete," Linda said. "You have a sweet, honest face—I noticed it right away. But you don't want to get caught in the middle of this mess. And you need to understand something about my Nora. The girl makes trouble wherever she goes. She thrives on it."

"She didn't make any trouble here," I said, although after I said it, I realized it wasn't true.

Linda straightened up and crossed her arms again, losing patience. "Well, she made enough trouble back home to last a lifetime. She had a fling with her stepdad, okay? My husband at the time. Are you listening? And she knew exactly what she was doing, too. She did it deliberately to hurt me. You really think you know this girl?"

"I know that when she came here, she was pretty messed up," I said evenly. "But I believe she's changed."

"Oh right, she's completely reformed. Give me a break. I hate to be the one to break it to you, but the girl is using you. She's using you and she's using her uncle too, although *he* deserves it. Nora is my daughter and I love her, but she uses people left and right."

I didn't back down. "I think spending time with Abe has changed her."

Linda threw up her hands. "God, you're such a romantic! People around here live in a dream world. Her father was the same way—just so blind about everything. And so obsessed with this place. Over-the-moon about a stupid, muddy river. But you know what—he loved *me*! He would have done anything for me. He was going to build me my dream house right on this river. And he sure as hell wouldn't have wanted me to end up with nothing when he died. These small-minded people around here, they just couldn't understand that."

I looked down at my hands on the desk. The office hummed with my refusal to respond. Linda picked up a tiny bat skull from my desktop. I thought for a moment that she might throw it against a wall, but instead she put it gingerly back down on the desk and gave me her more calculated smile again. "Okay, Big Guy, here's the deal. Here's what you need to tell our girl. Tell her I'll give her another day or two to think about whatever it is she needs to think about. If that's what's required, I can handle it. I'll stay at Rita's. Let me give you the phone number there."

She rummaged in her purse for a pen and a scrap of paper, scribbled a phone number, and set the note on one corner of my desk. "When will you be talking to her?"

"I don't know, Mrs. Cobb."

"Call me Linda. When do you *think* you'll be talking to her?"

"It's up to her at this point. I'll see her if she ... appears."

"Appears?" Linda repeated. "Oh, she'll appear all right. She'll be wanting something from you, don't you worry. And when she does, you give her that number and tell her I'm still here and I'm not leaving without her."

Then she was gone. The fan clattered in the silence. I took a few deep breaths, then opened the drawer of my desk and took out the note Nora had left me during the night.

I couldn't tell you before. I was too afraid it would make you change your mind about me. Please don't tell Abe. And tell him not to look for me. I'm okay. I just need to hide for a while. Love, Nora.

———

Abe drove up in the jeep and lumbered into the office, rumpled, unshaven, and walking with a dip in his step because he was carrying a heavy metal case by its handle. A familiar metal case—the moth collection. He set the case on his own desk and turned to me. "I know it sounds crazy," he said, "but I can't stand these … things."

"They're *moths*, Abe."

"Well, I can't have them in the house if she's leaving."

"Are you sure she's leaving?"

Abe gave me the totally defeated look again. "Why would she want to stay with me now?"

"Your brother's death was a freak accident," I said patiently. "Trust me, it doesn't change how Nora feels about you."

"It was her dad," Abe argued softly. "The father she never got to know. And he died because of me."

I didn't know what to say to this; I just shook my head.

"Have you talked to her?" he asked.

"No, but I got a note from her this morning," I told him. "She's okay. She's camping on the river. But she's hiding because of something else. Something that happened before she came here."

"You mean the thing with her stepdad?" he asked.

My jaw dropped. "You *know*?"

"I didn't know. I just … I suspected. There was something about the way she wouldn't talk about him. Wouldn't even say his name. I had a bad feeling about it. It was one of the reasons I felt so strongly about not sending her back to Indianapolis. I wanted to … protect her."

His voice broke—a sob had caught him off guard. He

lowered himself into his chair and covered his face. I wanted to steady him. I walked over to where he was sitting and put a firm hand on his shoulder, as he had done so many times with me. After a moment, he uncovered his face and made an effort to pull himself together. "Oh, God," he sighed. "I don't know what to do with myself. When are Bella and Christina coming in?"

"Bella's in Chicago, remember? I don't know about Christina."

"I wish she'd come in," he said mournfully.

"Abe, she's in the phone book."

He pretended not to hear this; instead, he stood up and began searching around the office for his hat. "I need to walk. Yeah, maybe I'll just check the trails out this morning, see what I can see."

Go ahead, I replied silently. *Let Nora see you. She needs to know that you're still King of Riverside. No matter what happened fifteen years ago. No matter what you said the night your brother died.*

———

I took the moths downstairs, to my studio, to see what secrets they still held for me. *Luna, Imperial, Polyphemus, Promethea, Isabella Tiger*. One broken case, one tattered moth—the sad *Cecropia*. I handled the cases carefully. My feelings about them had not changed. I laid them flat on my drawing table to admire them. An hour passed in an instant.

As I began to restack them in the crate, I noticed an oddly loose corner inside the top of the metal lid; an old piece of gray cardboard had broken free. When I gave the cardboard the gentlest tug, it came out farther, and I saw that it was the backside of a framed certificate—a first-place certificate from the Department of Education of the State of Michigan, signed by the governor.

But there was more. Jammed underneath the certificate was an old notebook—a thin spiral that had been clamped into place under the certificate frame. I pulled it out carefully, placed it on my table and stared at it in amazement. *Moth Journal, 1988–1989*, the cover read. *Paul Thomas McMichael.*

It was quite a read. A few months of careful, passionate notes by someone I shared many things in common with: love for a place called Riverside, gratitude to a certain science teacher, fascination with moths and their lore, disinterest in superficial friendships. And in those very last entries, deep longing for a girl who would walk beside him and understand him and not see him in light of the tragedy in his life.

And not one single sentence, not a blessed word, about a mother.

———

Christina answered her doorbell in a flowered tent of a dress, and because I had never seen her in anything but jeans and old overalls, the first thing I said to her was, "Where are you going?"

"Dear boy," she said. "It's eight thirty in the morning. This is a housedress."

"I just … I've never seen you in a dress before."

"We're in a heat wave—haven't you noticed? It's way too hot for jeans." She pointed with disapproval at mine.

"I don't have any housedresses," I said, and she threw back her head and barked with laughter. It was so great to hear somebody flat-out laughing that I could have stood on her porch for the rest of the morning just to keep hearing it. But she waved me inside, still giggling, and I followed her into her kitchen.

"Do you want coffee?" she asked.

I said yes. She led me onto a small deck off the kitchen, where I viewed the far side of her subdivision. Across a fake pond were about twenty other pre-fab houses—no trees, no shade anywhere except the red and green canvas umbrellas over the patio tables on neighboring decks. Christina adjusted her umbrella to block the already hot sun. *No wonder she loves coming to Riverside,* I thought. I asked her if she'd heard anything from Bella.

"She called me yesterday," Christina said. "And it's even hotter in Chicago than it is here. Her dad thinks it's too hot to do anything and she's *painfully* bored. Forgive me, but that is music to my ears."

She sat down across from me and rested her chin in her hands. "But that's not why you're here, is it, Pete? To talk about Bella?"

"I needed to tell you about a few things that have happened since you stopped coming out."

"I know some of them. A certain female visitor. Sounds like you've all had quite a blast from the past."

"Who told you?"

"Nora did. She rode Abe's bike all the way from Riverside last night. It took her over two hours. I made her take a shower, eat some real food, sleep in Bella's bed. But before I woke up this morning, she was gone again."

"You're lucky. No one else has even seen her."

"Well, she's just fine, Pete. She really is. Although you should have seen the filthy clothes on her. They're soaking in my laundry tub. I gave her a couple of clean outfits and a different pair of boots." She pointed to a corner of the deck, where Nora's stained and muddy work boots sat. I recognized them with a pang.

"Did she tell you what her mom said about the night Paul McMichael died?"

"I heard the whole story. And man, do I wish I'd been there. I would have given that woman a run for her money! She would have had to knock me down first, to go after Abe like that. And saying those awful things right in front of Nora."

She took a calming breath, settling her anger. For a moment, I pictured it—Christina with her wild hair, putting herself between Linda and Abe. It made me smile.

Christina noticed. "You think I'm kidding?"

"No, I was just thinking that I wish you *had* been there."

"Honestly, as if that man hasn't been through enough in his lifetime!"

"Nora's mom is still here," I told her.

"Believe me, I know. The woman calls night and day. Nora left her cell phone here to charge, and there will probably be fifteen new messages from just this morning. Mom is on the warpath, but Nora's not ready to deal with Mom. And no wonder. I heard all about the creepy stepdad, too. Sounds like Mom's taste in men took a big nosedive after she left Buchanan."

I was relieved that she knew. "But there's something I don't understand, Christina," I said. "Why would Nora even consider leaving with her mom? She can stay with Abe as long as she wants to—she knows that. It just … it doesn't make sense to me."

"It's that mother-daughter thing, Pete," she said. "It goes way, way deep. And no, it doesn't always make sense to somebody on the outside looking in." She reached across the table and pressed my hand, a brief gesture of sympathy that ordinarily I would have shrank from.

"So … are you saying you think Nora *should* leave? Even after how her mom treated her? And treated Abe?"

"Pete, Nora will be *back*. She's a McMichael now! She's not finished with us. I'd put money on it, if I had any."

"I just don't think she should go," I said. "It seems like running away."

"No, it's way more complicated than running away. She

needs to make peace with her mother, if it's at all possible. She needs to try." Pressing my hand again. "But you'll miss her terribly, won't you?"

I wasn't willing to talk about missing Nora. "I have something else to ask you," I said. "I think Abe would really appreciate seeing you. I think you could help him."

"What makes you think Abe would accept my help, Pete? He hasn't given me any signals that he wants it."

"He's been missing you," I insisted. "There are ... signs."

She sighed. "I know the signs, Pete. Believe me, I've been watching for them for months. But at my age, I have to be realistic. I'm not a teenager anymore, no offense."

"You shouldn't give up. Try a new strategy. Nora says it's best to be really direct with Abe."

"I'm not Nora," she argued softly. "I'm not *family*. I'm just a person who comes out to Riverside to shovel bark and change the coffee filters. Maybe he thinks I'm too old for him."

"No, Christina. I'm sure he likes you!"

Christina covered her face with one hand, as though I had told her something upsetting. After a moment, she uncovered it. "Let's get back to how you feel about Nora leaving," she said. "Are you afraid she'll forget you? Get another boyfriend, make a bunch of new mistakes once she's out of your sight? Or are you more afraid that if she goes away, you'll forget *her*? Because that's what you do, isn't it? You move ahead in a straight line and you don't look back—am I right? Is that something else you learned from Abe?"

I took note of her dead-on accuracy. "Wow," I said. "Have you been talking to my gram?"

"I don't really know your gram, Pete. I never did the science thing in high school. I knew some kids who joined her after-school club and became her followers. She was kind of a nature guru for a lot of kids. But that just wasn't me. I never joined any high school clubs—I was too rebellious."

"My mom was one of Gram's favorites," I said.

Christina's eyes widened. "Your mom?"

"That's why she came back to Buchanan for help."

"You mean … after she had you?"

I nodded. "She looked up her old favorite teacher and Gram took her in."

"I've always wondered what the deal was with your mom, but it seemed like you didn't want to talk about it."

"I didn't," I said. But then I added, impulsively, "She knew Paul. They like … *knew* each other. They were seeing each other."

"You mean … oh for heaven's sake—are you sure?"

"I'm totally sure."

"I never knew that. That's a little unsettling, isn't it? Does Abe know?"

"I don't know," I said. "We could go ask him right now …"

She shook her head. "I'm not going to Riverside, Pete. I'm feeling just a little too … fragile."

"Right, whatever." I finished my coffee, disappointed that I hadn't convinced her about Abe. But at the same time, it felt good to have told her a bit of my own history. Surprisingly, solidly good. Before I left, Christina bagged up some of Bella's cereal and a few other things from her fridge, gave me Nora's charged cell phone, and thanked me for stopping by.

At the office was another note. *I'm afraid you'll think I'm running away. But I'm not. This is different. I need you to believe me. Do you believe me? What you think about me matters so much. Love, Nora*

Moth Journal

Paul McMichael

Buchanan, Michigan

February 1989

I will put the moths away, toss the leftover chemi-
cals, get rid of the jars, give back the microscope and
the books and the articles and the notes and the certificate and the rest of it, and focus my attention on
Abe. Abe needs me to help him get through the first
winter on our own. I will concentrate on him now and
teach him things and help him with his homework
and take him sledding a few more times and take him
down to the river when it thaws. It will be like the old
days—almost. We have so much to do, so much ahead
of us now. We will be the overseers, the two brothers
of Riverside in our silver canoe, the great explorers.
After I graduate we will decide how and when to make

Riverside our new home. It will be so good for both of us to leave this old house behind.

Winter will be over soon, the longest winter of my life. The winter of moths in cases, and science projects and funeral arrangements and Mrs. Shelton always watching me for signs of weakness. But I don't feel weak. I survived and persisted and won, and the winter is ending. Spring will bring graduation and freedom and love. I will walk the trails with Abe and Rose and Peter. If she will only stay. I want so much for her to be happy here and join me in my new life and stay.

Please stay.

Beautiful eyes of so many colors, dark hair, secret plans—who are you? Who did you love before you came here? Do you still love him? Can you turn away from him and learn to love me?

There is something I need. There is no need to wait. I've decided to buy myself a truck. I already have my eye on one—a dream of a truck, a white Chevy with a deep bed and wide tires and a beautiful grill. A truck to drive Abe around in and let him honk the horn and wave at other truck drivers. Will Rose be impressed? Would a shiny new truck convince her that I'm not too young for her?

My acceptance letter from Michigan State came in the mail yesterday. I've been nominated for a huge scholarship, all expenses paid, probably because of my success at the state science fair. A great honor, Mrs. Shelton says. But how can I possibly leave Abe? And now there is Rose—I don't know what she will decide, but I am at her mercy until she does, although I have promised not to pressure her. And how can I even think about leaving Buchanan? How can I leave Riverside now? A feeling is growing inside of me, a certainty that I need to stay. It feels like a relief to let the words come out onto the paper, to accept them: My life is here. I won't leave.

15. Missing Mothers

Dear Pete, I'm going to change my name. Or I should say, change my name back. I think my mother should too since she obviously never got over my dad. Did you know my middle name is Rose? It's such a coincidence—my middle name is your mother's name! Love, Nora

I heard a car pull up and I braced myself, but no one came inside. I approached the office window and saw that Linda was standing very still at the side of my truck. She'd placed both her hands on the driver's side door and lowered her head slightly, so that her black hair fell forward, covering her face. But I could tell she was upset—the air was charged with emotion.

I strongly considered sneaking down to the basement,

even locking myself in the studio, when she looked up and caught my shadow at the office window. "Pete Shelton!" she cried. "Come out here this minute and tell me where the hell you got this truck!"

I had no choice. I wandered out.

"Do you know whose truck this was?" she demanded.

"Nobody told me until a few weeks ago."

"We drove all over this *county* in this truck! We took our *honeymoon* in this truck! We drove up north. We drove down south. We drove for days on end. Nora was conceived in it! What in hell is it still *doing* here?"

"Abe gave it to my grandfather. Gramps gave it to me."

"Oh my God, whatever you do, don't tell Nora!"

"She already knows."

When I told her this, something snapped in her; her face completely collapsed like a child's. She covered her eyes with her hands and gave a high-pitched wail. "How can she stand it?" she cried. "How can she stand seeing it? Because I can't! I can't, I can't, I can't!"

"Mrs. Cobb—Linda—do you want to come inside and sit down?"

But she didn't move. "I can't stay another night in this awful place! It's torture for me. It's like he's still here. He's all around—I feel him. I can't leave Nora, but I can't stay. Why is this happening to me?"

She looked skyward and shook her fists. "What kind of a twenty-year-old man has a will that shuts out his own wife! Did he know he was going to die?"

"It was because of his mother." I said. "She left him in charge of Abe."

She looked at me as if I had said something cruel, and began to cry again.

"Look, would you just come inside a minute?" I pleaded.

She followed me in and I pulled out my desk chair for her to sit on and brought her a glass of water. I noticed that she was sitting in her chair awkwardly, arching her spine and struggling to get comfortable. "My back is out," she said. "I'm sleeping on the world's oldest sleeper sofa, I swear. I haven't had a decent night's sleep since I got here. I just lie awake on that lumpy mattress and all these memories come flying at me. Just flying at me. Like they've been waiting for me all these years, preserved in this awful town."

She was wearing a pair of cheap athletic shoes that looked too big for her. When she saw me staring at them, she said, "They're Rita's. I borrowed them because I thought ... I thought maybe I would walk down to the river and see if I could find Nora myself. What do you think?"

"I think she'll see you long before you see her."

"I want her to see me! Maybe if she knows I'm trying to find her, she'll have mercy on me. Can you help me get down there, Pete? Point me in the right direction? It's been quite a while and I never did pay any attention to directions around here."

It was hard for me to imagine her walking to the river alone, even on trails with clear markers. "Let me get you some repellent," I said, rummaging through my desk drawer.

I pulled out a scrap of paper and added, "I'll draw you a little map."

———

I watched her walking away, her small frame disappearing down the Main Trail. I don't know why exactly, but I had an overwhelming impulse to follow her. To keep track of her and make sure that she made it in one piece to the river. So I changed my own shoes, sprayed my shoulders and back with repellent, waited another ten minutes, and then took off behind her.

It was only about ten in the morning, but already stifling. A thin breeze lifted from the warm river. The trees along the trail drooped like wilting umbrellas. I headed for the crest that showed the longest view of the river—the ridge behind Elnora's Point, the same spot from which Bella had probably watched me kissing Nora. At the top of the crest I could see Elnora's Point clearly.

Linda was lying on the bench at Elnora's Point. She was curled up like a child on the narrow boards, her arms covering her face. Even from that distance, I was pretty sure she was weeping, undone by heat and fatigue and memories. I watched her until my attention was drawn to the amazing sight of an adult bald eagle, with its snow-white head, lifting slowly into flight from the top of a tree on the other side of the river.

And then I noticed the metallic glint of the canoe, just north of me, on the opposite bank. And through the trees I caught the merest flash of blue—a color that quickly changed into a person, someone emerging on the opposite crest, a girl, a beloved girl in a blue T-shirt, her hair bleached to a wild, metallic orange. Nora, unseen by her mother but seen by me. I wanted her to see me back, so I stepped out of the trees into a small clearing and waited for her eyes to also track the eagle—it was heading toward me—and find me standing at attention across the river from her.

Which she did. She saw me. And then we were looking at each other with the river between us, Elnora's Point below us. I could not see Nora's face clearly, but as I gazed at her, she made the slightest gesture—she lifted her hand to the side of her head and then opened it in a motionless wave. I did the same. Then she pointed downward and across the river, to her mother. And I did the same. I felt, in that moment, that Nora and I were the two old souls of the river and Linda was the orphan child.

I felt this glimmer of understanding. Or rather, I understood that there was something in the world that I would never understand. The bond between a living child and a living mother, something that, as Christina had said, went way, way deep. I would never know it. The unknowable deepness of it.

I also felt Nora's absence coming toward me. Yet I was feeling closer to her than I had ever felt before. She would leave me. I would miss her. I would not refuse to miss her, I would choose to miss her. I would not put the summer we had shared behind me. I wouldn't bury it. I would hold it with me, endure her absence, and hope for her return.

After she disappeared from view, I saw Linda pull herself upright on the bench and wipe her eyes with the backs of her hands. I left the crest and hurried back to the office to make a pitcher of iced tea. I suspected that Linda would return in worse shape than when she'd arrived. I wanted to be as helpful as possible. She wasn't just some stranger in bad shoes who'd walked down to the river, after all. She was my girlfriend's mother.

———

On my way home, I stopped at the cabin to ask Abe an important new question. I quickly saw that I had interrupted a conversation between him and Christina. They were sitting side by side on the top step of Abe's porch, Abe with his elbows on his knees, Christina leaning close and listening to whatever he was saying. I glanced around the drive; there was no sign of Christina's car. As I came closer, I could read in Abe's face that he was embarrassed to have been caught in this moment, but Christina smiled and waved me over. I hopped out of the truck and walked toward them.

"Do you two need a moment?" Christina asked. "Shall I wait inside?" Then she met my eyes and rolled hers meaningfully.

"Maybe just a few," Abe agreed softly.

Christina stood up, straightened her skirt, and disappeared behind the screen door.

"How'd she get over here?" I couldn't help asking.

"I went and got her," Abe said gruffly. "I had something

I needed to talk to her about. What are you doing here, anyway?"

"I have something I need to ask you," I said. "It's about Rose."

"Rose?" he repeated. "You mean ... your mom Rose?"

I nodded. "She lived with Gram and Gramps for a little while before you did. And your brother knew her. Did you know that?"

"I knew she lived with Ida and Conrad," he said. "But ... you're saying she knew Paul?"

"You don't remember ever meeting a girl named Rose? A little older than Paul? With a baby?" I pointed to myself.

Abe lowered his head and rubbed his already messy hair. His grizzled chin. His stubbly red sideburns. He was trying hard to remember. "I might have met her," he said finally. "It is possible. There were quite a few girls that Paul knew ... before Linda came. But they're all kind of jumbled in my mind, Pete. Like everything else from that time."

"Abe, something else. After you moved in with us, didn't you ever ask Gram what had happened to my mom?"

"I think she probably told me. Way long ago. At least about her moving to Idaho."

"Didn't it ever seem weird to you that my mom did that? Ran away and left me behind?"

"People run away, Pete. All the time. My own dad left my mom just after I was born. And besides, the Sheltons were so glad to have you. We all were. You were the most awesome little kid. But why are you asking me this now?"

"Remember a while ago you said that there was this

emptiness in Paul when he met Linda? I'm pretty sure that the emptiness was because Rose left. He still needed her. And I just thought … I thought you might want to know that. That you were right on target about that emptiness thing."

"Pete," Abe asked softly. "Who in the world have you been talking to?"

"I have my sources," I said. "Don't worry about it." I stood up and dusted off the back of my jeans. *Don't worry about a damn thing ever again,* I added silently.

I left him alone with his new friend.

———

That night I drove back to Riverside before dark, bringing with me two fast food hamburgers in a bag and double fries—which I left on the kitchen table for the night flier, my moth girl.

Moth Journal

Paul McMichael

Buchanan, Michigan

February 1989

What will happen to the big silk moths? Will traffic and pollution make it impossible for males to follow the trail of pheromones to the females? Will pesticides kill them? Will their habitats disappear? Will house lights and street lights distract them and make mating impossible? Are they the dinosaurs of the insect world, huge and wonderful, but doomed?

Maybe Rose is right, and it was a strange way to spend half a year of my life, but I am glad that I preserved them. Perhaps some day—a long time from now—someone who hasn't seen a Cecropia or a Luna or a Prometheus in the wild will look at the ones I've put into cases and feel a glimmer of what I felt in the swamps and the basement and the laboratories before my collecting came to an end and I came back to my life and my future.

Then again, who knows? Maybe the moths of Riverside will outlast me! Maybe I'll start another collection in the spring! Maybe Rose will stay!

16. Funeral

Could you do something for me? Take the moths off the walls of my room and bring them to the river. I want to see them one more time. I'm leaving with Mom tomorrow. Will you tell Abe? Love, Nora

The ultraviolet lamp was still in a small storage room at the back of the garage, a place where Gram still kept many odds and ends from her years of teaching. I pulled the flat sheet off the top of my own bed. I packed a blanket. Insect repellent. Water. Paul's notebook. My pencils and a sketchpad—these went into my backpack. The metal specimen container went into the back of my truck.

Gram saw from the kitchen window that I was packing up for something; she came out to where my truck was parked. "Where are you taking my old field lamp, Peter?"

"It's only for tonight," I promised. "I'll put it right back where I found it in the morning."

"Will you be looking for moths?" she asked.

"It's a perfect night for it, don't you think? Full moon. No wind. Rain on the way. But I'm not turning into a moth-collector, Gram. I'm just going to the woods to see a few moths and say goodbye to Nora."

"So she's definitely leaving."

"She's definitely leaving. I hope she'll come back."

"I hope so too," Gram said softly. "My dear friend's beautiful grandchild."

I threw my backpack into the passenger side of my truck and shut the door. "Did my mom join a cult when she left here, Gram?"

Gram stiffened, but her voice remained calm and factual. "Some would call it a cult," she said. "If by cult you mean an exclusive system of religious attachment."

"Did somebody come and actually take her away?"

"Not by force, Peter," she said. "But she left very suddenly. We didn't actually meet the man she left with."

"Was he my father?"

"I doubt it," she said. "But we don't know for sure."

"Did Rose know you and Gramps would adopt me?"

"I like to think that she knew, son. But the fact remains, we never discussed it."

"And you never heard from her after that?"

"We tried to reach her. But we never heard anything back. Never, Peter. All that year and the year after. And then we accepted things exactly the way they were. And we were grateful. So … unspeakably grateful.

"But what about Paul?" I asked.

"Paul?" she repeated. "Who told you about Rose and Paul? I didn't think Abe knew."

"He doesn't know. He doesn't remember. I found out another way. I'll tell you about it some time, Gram. After I've done a little more research on my own."

"Wait a minute. What sort of research?"

"Are you questioning my need to conduct research?" I asked, challenging her.

"Not at all. Research is key. Fact-finding is definitely in order. But this is not what I have come to expect from you. It's a bit of a change."

"Everybody else is changing," I said. "Why not me?"

"Why not you, indeed!"

"I don't want anyone to help me, Gram. I mean it. I want to do this my own way."

"I won't interfere. I won't speak of it unless I'm spoken to. Nor will Conrad."

I looked at the darkening sky. "I'd better get going if I'm going to say goodbye to Nora before the rain comes."

"Carry on, then. Give the girl a hug for me." She gave me a little push, toward the cab of the truck, and I was off.

———

It *was* a perfect night for moths—moonlit and damp with the promise of rain, distant thunder in the wings, a downpour predicted before morning. I drove my truck to a familiar point near the river, the closest to the water I could get and still be surrounded by trees. Then I hoisted my backpack onto my shoulders and carried the metal crate with one hand. The other hand held a flashlight, searching for a spot that would enclose me but still be open enough for my light to be seen from a good distance away. This was my method. This was the night. I was the bait.

———

The combination of moonlight and artificial light, combined with the coming rain, made small moths gather from far and wide, a multitude of species and sizes, an urgent gathering. They were both disoriented and purposeful, weaving in and out of the light, casting oversized shadows against the stretched sheet until the sheet itself was a kind of puppet show, a shadow box, crazy with movement.

After about an hour, I began to sense that she was near. I sat very still. Soon a tall and wondrous creature came up behind me, put her lips against my cheek and covered my eyes with her calloused hands. I froze for a long moment, breathing her scent. Then stood up and turned around, blocking the light and causing moths to scatter. I wrapped my arms around her and pulled her close and kissed her.

"What did you bring me?" Nora asked.

"I brought the moths," I said. I hesitated. "And something else. Something that belongs to you. I brought it here to give you, but I'm afraid it will make you sad."

"I'm already sad," she said. "Show me."

I pulled the notebook out of my backpack and held it up to the light for her so that she could see the front cover. She gasped. "Where did you find this?"

"It was stuck in the lid of the moth crate," I explained. "It was there all the time. I discovered it yesterday."

"Is it his diary?" she asked.

"Actually, it's more about the moths."

"Then why would it make me sad?"

I couldn't answer her. She folded the notebook against her chest, lowering her head and thinking. Then she handed it back to me. "I can't take it now," she said. "Not now, when I'm going back. I need to save all my energy to be with my mom and my sister. I'll read it when I come back."

"When will that be?"

"I can't say, exactly. But this will be the proof that you'll see me again soon. You have my father's notebook. I have to read it. I can't wait to read it. But if reading it will make me sad, then I want you with me when that happens."

"Done," I said. "So, as you can see, I also brought pencils and a drawing pad. I want to draw your portrait. Sit over there, on that log with your back against the sheet."

She settled herself, arranged her legs, fluffed her already wild hair, and posed for me. I drew her with moth shadows circling her head, an orbiting halo. As I drew, she sifted through the moth crate, studying the collection and lifting her head from time to time to gaze at me, her eyes piercing. When she came to the broken *Cecropia*, she shook her head sadly.

"Something in me broke that day, too. Like a river washing over me—all the things nobody had ever told me. All the time with him I never had. I might have broken more of them if Abe hadn't been there to calm me down."

"Speaking of Abe, can you talk to him before you leave tomorrow?" I asked. "He needs to hear that you don't blame him for the accident."

"Oh God, Pete, how could he think that?"

"Because he blames himself. Nora, you were so right about him having a secret he couldn't tell us."

"It was his secret-beyond-all-forgiving," she said. "I had one, too."

"You know what, Nora? I'm starting to think that everybody has one."

"I think I know what yours is."

This made my breath catch in my throat. I looked up from my drawing, waiting for what she was going to say next. "Yours is about your mom."

I began drawing again. *The artist thing. You take after your mom. Did you ever see her again?* "I've decided that I'm going to find out more about her," I announced.

"I think that's a good idea, Pete. Based on certain personal experience."

I shrugged. "Maybe. Maybe not. I'm a little afraid of what I'll find out," I admitted.

"I know what you mean. Kind of like finally finding out about the night my dad died. But you know what? I'm glad I know. And I'm glad Abe was the one who finally told me."

I told her about finding Abe and Christina alone together on Abe's porch. She was, of course, thrilled.

"Give me details," she begged. "When you saw them, were their heads close together? Were they like face-to-face? No? Side by side? Were their hands touching?"

"Nora, they were away from Riverside! Alone together! That's enough of a miracle for now."

"A miracle," she agreed. "And hey, it might never have happened if my mom hadn't come here and gone so crazy on him."

I tore Nora's portrait from the pad with a flourish, walked over to where she was sitting, and held it in front of her eyes for her to admire.

"Can I keep it?" she asked. "Please? To remind me of this night?"

I gave her the near-empty sketchpad to protect the drawing and put my pencils and the notebook back into my pack. While I was doing this, Nora came up behind me and wrapped her arms around my waist. Her T-shirt held the smell of grass and campfire and her own unmistakable scent. Her hair was musky and soft, her skin slightly damp. Pheromones. I turned, and her mouth was mine.

Distant thunder was growing louder; we both knew we had to get out of the woods soon. "Take me to Abe's," Nora said. "I'll stay with him tonight and call my mom in the morning."

I offered to help her take down her campsite; she led me to it and together we began packing up her equipment. "I've been thinking about the moth collection," she said. "Even after I put them up on my wall, I was starting to feel strange about them. They're so dead, Pete. Captured and pinned and just very, very dead."

"I think that's how Abe feels about them."

"He's so soft-hearted. He could never stick a pin in a bug. He wouldn't hurt any living creature. Man, how stupid to choose him to hate him forever. I'm really going to have to work on her about that."

We were both leaning against the side of the truck and I pulled her close and kissed her and buried my face for a moment in her hair … thinking of how much I was going to miss her, miss the curve of her neck and the soft hollow where her neck met her shoulder. "I'll keep the moths safe for you," I whispered.

But she shook her head. "I'm trying to say that I don't want them anymore. I want you to have them back. Do you still want them?"

"I think they belong at Riverside. It's what your dad would have wanted. I'll finish drawing them and then I'll make a display for one of the classrooms. It will give me something else to do while you're gone. So I won't miss you."

"It won't work."

"Right. I know."

"And what about the one I broke?" she asked.

"The *Cecropia*? It's not salvageable. It's turning to dust."

"We should bury it. Let's bury it in the river."

"Now?"

"Sure, it won't take long," she said. "The canoe is close by and it's not raining yet."

We opened the crate again. The broken case was right on the top; we pulled out the huge, disintegrating silk moth. Nora separated the frame from the backing, pulled out the remaining pins, and let the moth remains flutter into her open hand.

She hurried ahead of me, rushing to beat the storm. We pushed the canoe out in water up to our knees; Nora hopped in and I followed. I quickly rowed us to the middle of the river while Nora cradled the *Cecropia* in her hands. The first moth, King of *Saturnidae*, huge and silent and disappearing, the creature that had started it all.

When the first drops hit us, she let go of the papery corpse. It settled onto the surface of the water, and we watched it float away, raindrops dotting the water around us.

"Goodbye, goodbye," Nora called. "You old muddy river—go ahead and miss me!"

She pulled the second set of oars from the floor of the canoe and we rowed back to shore, where we ran to the old truck in a deluge.

The End

The Moths of Riverside

Collected and mounted by Paul McMichael,
Buchanan High School, Buchanan, Michigan, 1988–89.
All specimens found in the swamps and clearings along the
St. Joseph River, between East River Road and Winn Road.

Family of Sphingidae

Twin-Spotted Sphinx—*wingspan 3 inches (blue hindwing eye-*
spots, unusual forewing margins)

White Lined Sphinx—*wingspan 3¼ inches (distinctly patterned*
and margined; feeds on honeysuckle)

Hummingbird Clearwing—*wingspan 2 inches (clear patches on*
wings give the impression of holes)

Family of Noctuidae

Ilia Underwing—*wingspan 3 inches (yellow hindwing flash of*
color to startle predators; feeds on oak foliage)

Brown Hooded Owlet—*wingspan 2 inches (unusual streamlined*
appearance of folded wings when at rest)

Variegated Cutworm—*wingspan 2 inches (notorious pest! Hidden beauty in pearlescent brown forewings and hindwings)*

Family of Saturnidae

Promethea—*wingspan 3 inches (plain, large, and slow flying—easy to catch)*

Automeris Io—*wingspan 5½ inches (called "bulls-eye" moth because of markings, striking blue eyespots)*

Yellow Imperial—*wingspan 5½ inches (large, yellow wings; can be as large as 7 inches!)*

Cecropia—*wingspan 6 inches (my largest moth! Many eyespots and distinct silver patches at forewing tip; males larger than females)*

Polyphemus—*wingspan 4½ inches (large, common, and beautiful; large gray and yellow eyespots, distinctly feathered antennae)*

Luna—*wingspan 5 inches (unique color, green, ghostly, large furry body, amazing antennae; sexes similar)*

Family of Notodontidae

Morning Glory Prominent—*wingspan 2 inches (ordinary brown, beautiful under a microscope; males smaller than females)*

Family of Geometridae

Tulip Tree Beauty—*wingspan 2 inches (distinctively scalloped hindwing edge; males smaller than females)*

Red-headed Inchworm—*wingspan 1½ inches (unique chocolate brown patches on the forewings)*

Large Maple Spanworm—wingspan 2 inches (distinctive tail projections on the hindwings)

Family of Arctidae

Isabella Tiger—wingspan 2½ inches (hardy moth; forewings pale orange-yellow to orange-brown, black spots toward wingtips)

All moths are displayed in separate display cases, except:

4 in one case: **Maple Spanworm**
Variegated Cutworm
Red-headed Inchworm
Morning Glory Prominent

3 in one case: **Hummingbird Clearwing**
Brown Hooded Owlet
Tulip Tree Beauty

About the Author

Margaret Willey has written many books for children, including *Clever Beatrice*, winner of the Charlotte Zolotow Award, and the young adult novel *Facing the Music*. Her most recent book for children is *The 3 Bears and Goldilocks*. She grew up in southwestern Michigan, where she now lives, indulging in various obsessions: silk moths, owls, and folktales. Visit Margaret online at www.SummerOfSilkMoths.com.